Tales of No Pretence

Cornelia Ramsay

Sydney Australia

Cornelia Ramsay c/- Intertype Publish and Print
Unit 45, 125 Highbury Road
BURWOOD VIC 3125
Australia
www.intertype.com.au

Ordering Information:
Quantity sales. Special discounts are available on quantity purchases by corporations, associations, and others. For details, contact the "Special Sales Department" at the address above.

Tales of No Pretence / Cornelia Ramsay. —1st ed.
ISBN 978-1-7635027-5-8

To my wonderful husband, Ray, and brilliant daughter, Crina,
for their unwavering belief and never-ending support.
To Sharon for editing the stories and for her continuous
support and feedback.
To Bobby for helping me bring my dream into reality.
To Lee for the matter-of-fact feedback.
To Asiyeh for the beautiful illustrations.

"I had the pleasure of being among the first readers of 'Tales of No Pretence', a collection of short stories by Cornelia Ramsay. Cornelia's writing style is very accessible, and her stories are engrossing. The stories run across a range of genres with a couple of them having the feel of an Edgar Allen Poe short story in a more modern context while others feel semi-autobiographical. The characters and events Cornelia writes about are very relatable and some of her stories had me on the edge of my seat in anticipation. There's something for everyone in this collection and, like me, the readers will probably be unable to put the book down till they reach the end of a story"...**Sharon Luhr**

"Stories connect. They connect time, place, culture and self. They connect the reader to the protagonist and the protagonist to the author. To fully immerse oneself in a story it is necessary to share a little of oneself to connect. That act can, for many of us, be challenging. To write a story, one must share all of oneself and open a window to experiences only the writer has and portray them in a manner that bring others closer to that personal and hidden, journey. This collection does that, and not by opening a window to a world of fantasy and magic, but rather a window into grit and resilience, encounters and unresolved questions that can only be experienced through the lens of one's own journey."...**Lee Styger**

Contents

The Café No More

A young couple find themselves in the middle of a terrifying
incident that plunges them into a fight for survival.

The café was full.

Mark's hands were shaking, whether from the bitter cold outside or nicotine withdrawal. Dirty habit.

He was trying to convince himself he'd be okay with Anna, a fellow university student, whose eyes seemed unnaturally green as they stood in the doorway. She was a bit of a stunner, she had brown hair, a beautiful smile and a slim figure. The only catch was she was almost the same height as he was and had, he suspected, a sharpish intellect. He wasn't sure how his rather pedestrian maths and chemistry would match up with her major in French.

He'd had an eye on her for a while now. ...So did many other guys.

Last Saturday, he had accidentally bumped into her at a student club. During a brief lull in the conversation, he had mustered the courage to take the plunge, uttering words he had practiced meticulously and knew by heart. Despite his preparation, he had still stumbled.

"How about coffee on Monday?"

"Sure," she laughed.

He had felt flattered at the time, but now, anxiety had kicked in. All his friends had girlfriends, with some even moving in together. He felt like he was falling behind.

The past few days had been a roller coaster of emotions. He couldn't help but wonder how he would measure up.

Inside the café, disaster. Not a table in sight.

"There, on the back wall," she nudged.

She was sharp.

They scrambled through. Those eyes. She radiated not only intelligence but also an enduring charm that left him almost breathless as she gracefully unravelled her scarf.

"Tea, coffee, er ..." he stumbled.

"Tea and whatever, please" she said.

He threaded through the crowd to place their order.

The tea took a long time to arrive. He discreetly glanced back in the direction he had just come from.

She was sitting calmly giving him the once-over from the ground up when she experienced a sudden flashback. Last Saturday, at the club, she had strategically positioned herself close to him. This guy was a bit reserved, with dark hair and eyes, a well-built physique, and a similar height to her. He didn't seem like the overly assertive type, which was a relief for Anna, as she had moved past her attraction to such individuals.

"One hot tea, mud cake and a hot chocolate for me," said Mark putting down the tray.

Suddenly, seemingly from nowhere, a couple emerged.

"Mind if we sit with you?" asked the guy who sported a red nose and flashed a superb set of pearlies. On his arm a sexy, tall brunette.

Mark attempted an open mouth. The place was crowded, what could he say.

"Join us, no problem," Anna got in first.

Mark kept quiet. ... So much for a table for two...

The brunette sat down beside Anna revealing a radiant smile:

"Hi, I'm Helen".

"Anna". They shook hands.

"Your hot chocolate is getting cold, Mark," said Anna. "Not exactly sociable, this bloke," Anna thought.

"Where are my manners," Alan butted in "I'm Alan and happy as hell'.

"Has it got to do with that beautiful ring on Helen's hand?" joked Anna.

"How did you know?" Alan replied, staring at Helen.

"No, it's a woman's thing, don't worry about it" said Anna smiling back at Helen. "Congratulations!"

"Am I missing something here?" clicked in Mark.

"Helen and I are engaged, I just proposed to her tonight" explained Alan, his eyes sparkling.

Mark choked. What was Anna, a psychic?

"Wow, that's a nice pendant," continued Helen looking at Anna playfully.

Mark observed as Anna's hand came to rest on her chic heart-shaped pendant, which gleamed brilliantly. He knew he needed to be careful.

"It's called L'Amour. My mother gave it to me," a twinkle in her eye.

Mark was pretending to check his wallet, or at least that's what it appeared. The word "love" or "l'amour", in French, made him feel a bit nervous. He could not help but wonder, if this was a test.

"I tell you what, why don't we all celebrate this special moment with a nice glass of champagne?" blurted Alan. "Anyone in?"

Hands shot up immediately. Mark was the last to raise his.

Alan stood up and swivelled towards the counter.

"Whoops!" he giggled as he bumped the table. Anna's right hand snatched at her cup to hold it in place while her left arm grounded the table. The little pendant slipped down her neck in the sudden twist, then plunged to the floor. The cups wobbled and spilt a few drops.

"I've got it" said Mark, snaking under the table, picking it up.

The girls were busy wiping away the spills on the table. Well, what could you expect from men? They exchanged knowing glances.

"Sorry about that, guys. I'll bring more serviettes" said Alan and squeezed through the crowd to the café counter. His black leather jacket, squeaky clean jeans and athletic figure lingered on Mark's mind. Would that be Anna's preferred type?

Suddenly the table started to tremble, this time causing the teaspoons to dance in the saucers. In seconds it turned into a more serious rumble, like a high-powered car at idle. Anna and Helen stopped wiping and stared, alarmed, at each other. They held their breath.

As his chair trembled, Mark glanced out the window, attempting to understand the cause of the commotion. Then, he locked eyes with Alan at the counter, who appeared to be in a state of desperation.

A deep groan emanated from within the café, a crescendo of concrete on steel, growing louder and louder until it became a muffled grumble right under their feet.

People jumped up, wildly turning their heads in all directions, utter confusion on some faces, sheer terror on others. Everyone stared at the walls and floor of the café. One mirror cracked then another. Somewhere somebody cried: "Earthquake! Run!"

At that moment the lights went out followed by a split second of dead silence. The silence then erupted in an aria of shrieking terror and all hell broke loose.

Alan raced across to them from the counter. Helen clutched frantically at him. Mark grabbed Anna's hand in a firm grip and yelled "This way." They made for the only exit, Helen, and Alan in close pursuit.

The building started to shake violently. The screech of steel girders rang through the confined space compounding the banshee, shattering the relative calm that had prevailed only minutes beforehand. The avalanche of panic grew uncontrollable.

Mark stepped gingerly over obstacles in the dark room, almost falling over. He regained his balance and roared "Annaaa."

"I'm right behind you," she replied in a tight voice.

People started to push and tumble but jammed at the exit door. "Oh my God!" several voices screamed repeatedly. "Run, run, the building is collapsing."

The main support pillars of the café creaked and groaned showering powdered dust and debris.

Mark pushed on through the chaos and finally managed to reach the front bay windows of the café bar near the entrance door. In the intense gloom he felt around, found the metal back of a chair, grabbed it and swung it with all his might at the nearest window. But to no effect. Desperately he swung the chair again, hoping against all odds it would break the window.

"I'm not going out like this," and he swung the chair again and again and again.

Finally, he heard the cracking of glass and the window shattered under his final adrenalin-driven blast, helped no doubt by the earthquake which continued to rumble. Something warm was running down his face. It had a salty taste. A sharp pain ignited in his right arm, but he ignored it. Mark paused to gather his senses. He had achieved an escape route. Anna's breath was coming hot and heavy on the back of his neck.

People were crying and crawling in despair all around them.

"That's our only way of escape," he shouted, measuring up the window. He clutched a handful of one of Anna's sleeves from behind, lifted his other arm to shield his face from the glass, and counted aloud, "One. Two. Three. Jump."

He caught the edge of the pavement with his right knee. Excruciating pain. The cold of the night blasted through his thin cotton shirt. Unconsciously shivered but didn't let go of Anna's arm.

Terrified cries of those still trapped inside invaded the night but he saw nothing. Dust filled his nostrils, and he began coughing up debris.

Silence followed, deathly silence. For a moment, he thought he was dreaming.

Then he heard the girl's weeping.

"Anna?" he whispered gently, "Are you OK?" he asked turning to the figure that lay inches behind his bruised and bleeding legs.

The girl didn't answer but kept crying quietly, her arm shaking in shock, her blouse shredded.

"Anna, please, are you OK?" he persisted.

The sharp stabbing pain in his knee forced him to collapse beside her. His hand slid from her arm to grasp at his ruined kneecap. He fumbled in the front pocket of his jeans, produced his trusty cigarette lighter and quickly thumbed the wheel. A small light flickered, and he strained to establish the identity of the person before him.

"Helen?" he asked anxiously "Are you alright? ...Where is Anna?"

A faint cry echoed in the night.

Mark gathered his ebbing strength and started crawling towards it. One crawl, one break, one more crawl and another break.

It seemed like ages. Then a breath came up to his face, shallow but steady. Anna's smell filled his sandy nostrils. She was lying on her back, in agony.

"Thank God! You're alive!" said Mark and cuddled her brown hair. With his lighter up, he ran a quick check over her body. Her eyes slowly flipped open:

"I can't move my left leg," she grunted.

"I'd say your thigh is broken, stay still, I'll get help," said Mark. He knelt down and held Anna's hand, his mind racing.

"Are you OK? Where are the others?" she squeaked.

"I'm over here," responded Helen through her sobs.

"Helen? Is that you?" blasted a male voice, hidden behind a bunch of rubble. The three heads turned in unison to the dark wobble ling silhouette that was attempting to stand up.

"Alan, my darling!" cried Helen and hopped to support him.

Only meters away, a deafening sound of falling debris, metal bending and a blast of energy knocked them all off their feet. The cafeteria was no more, just a pile of rubble fuming in the dark.

The cigarette lighter flickered and then extinguished. Mark shook it vigorously and repeatedly thumbed it until it ignited again, revealing a glimmer on the ground.

"I've found L'Amour," Mark declared. He picked up the pendant and handed it over to Anna, as he locked eyes with Anna's captivating green gaze.

Flight to Freedom

In the most challenging circumstances, the human spirit finds a way to rise.

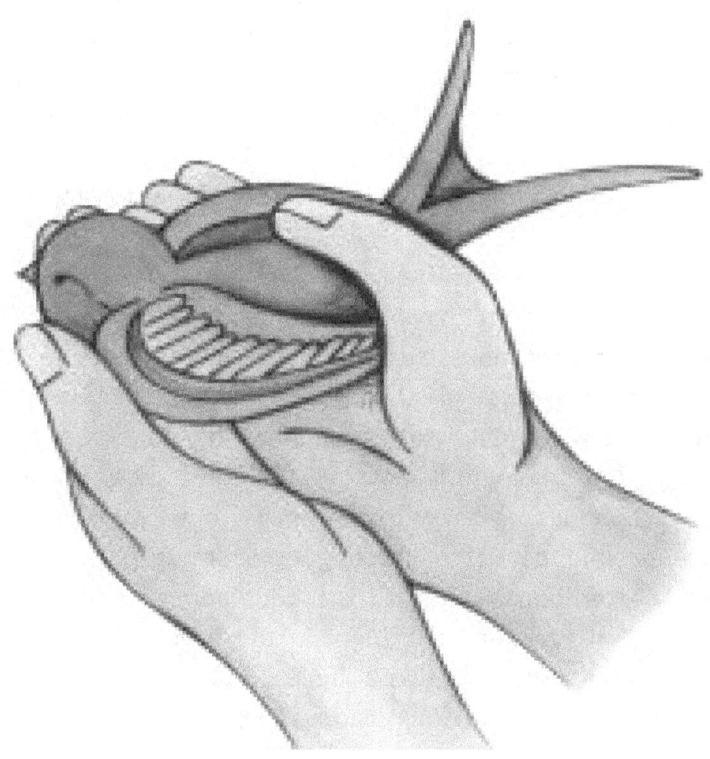

It was 1983 in Bucharest, Romania. A time when the communist regime was harsh and unforgiving, and when the state control and conformity were dictating our terms of living.

Imagine this: back in 1978 a big project called The Palace of Parliament had been commissioned to be built. The Communist Party leader wanted to make a statement to the world after that big nasty earthquake in '77 that shook the city to its foundations and took away so many lives.

So, they thought, "Why not copy North Korea's swanky palace in Pyongyang?" Easy peasy, right? Wrong! Many neighbourhoods, businesses, churches, hospitals, and schools were bulldozed to make way for the giant building. Forced labour and soldiers were in high demand and in the blink of an eye over 40,000 people were relocated against their will. And guess who footed the bill for this grandeur? Yep, you guessed it – the regular folks like us. Crippling austerity was the name of the game and it hit people hard, including myself. The population was dying of hunger and cold in their homes. No one cared.

We all had to march to the beat of conformity. Life was tougher than ever.

The hope for a better existence was fading away for young and old alike. People didn't have much to look for anymore. The days had become a monotonous blur, leaving them with little to anticipate. Yet, amidst this bleak existence, they found a small oasis of solace: Sunday afternoon television programs, the only artistic refuge of sporadic entertainment and wit into their otherwise grim lives.

Which brings us back to our small group of spirited university students who dared to challenge the status quo. Almost every Sunday afternoon, we defied the odds and appeared on national television, like a beacon of light in the lives of many. Our music wasn't just a melody, it was a lifeline, a breath of fresh air. People found us amusing, our songs captivating, and our presence a source of joy.

We didn't stop at television appearances. We ventured beyond, participating in concerts and song contests across the country. Our music breathed life into the hearts of those who had lost hope.

Such bold defiance came at a price though. Our actions were perpetually scrutinised by the ever-watchful State Secret Services. As creative and nonconformist young students, we cleverly navigated the treacherous waters of a rigid society while staying true to our deepest convictions and to our unwavering belief in a better tomorrow.

The authorities believed that anything remotely related to the Western world was like a bull in a china shop for our nation. But we, a group of determined and innovative souls, were not about to let our spirit be crushed.

That spring of 1983 was as beautiful as ever.

We were standing there, in Herastrau Park, in one of its famous alleys, waiting for instructions. A couple of directors from the State-sponsored television had asked George, our conductor, to set up a shoot in the park, for a Sunday afternoon show. The program was supposed to portray happy teens running freely on a green grassy meadow, under clear skies, singing a song about joy and hope. It was meant to distract people from their own hardships. In the triumphant finale, we were asked to wave red, yellow, and blue scarves to resemble our national flag. Classic communist propaganda.

Hundreds of pictures had been taken there over the years, in that same place, ironically called the "Freedom spot", as if the park did not have any other beautiful corners.

A shoot could take several hours to film, but we were hoping this one would be quick. It was cold outside, and we wanted to have some fun on our own. Not many people during those times could appear on national TV. All programs were tightly controlled. We felt privileged.

As we were standing dressed in lightweight, vaguely pink costumes, shivering in the chilly morning, a young couple ambled by, smiling at us. We were having fun rubbing each other's back, attempting to warm ourselves up. The lady was pushing a baby stroller, the man's arm around her shoulders.

I smiled back.

Squinting at the sun and with a chilly wind stroking our bare knees, we were ready to begin.

George, our 32-year-old conductor, slurred a joke. We laughed. He never cared about the TV directors' instructions, "the goodwill experts," even if without their approval the show wouldn't air. They corrected our everything: gestures, glances, undisciplined hair.

An earring that dared to swing away from the earlobe was immediately tucked in – such capitalist baubles were not permitted on national TV channel, lest they corrupt the minds and souls. Unruly hair had to be tamed flat or held at the back. Any resemblance in any shape or form to celebrities from the western world had to be erased immediately. No long hair, no beards, no moustaches. Women put away their rings, earrings, bracelets, and anything else that made them stand out from the crowd or express their own personality. Everybody ought to conform with the party's ruling. No exceptions.

Just as we reached the required number of participants to depict the joyous bunch romping about, as mandated by State TV guidelines, George's attention was drawn to a peculiar movement amidst the grass at his feet.

"Look, there" he exclaimed.

I followed his gaze.

A little swallow, almost frozen, had recently returned from warmer climates, and was trembling exhausted on the chilly earth. It could hardly stretch its wings. I felt sorry for it but didn't know what to do.

We watched its powerless struggle in silence.

Out of nowhere a cameraman charging up the hill nearly stepped on it. I held my breath. George cried out and pushed the guy aside. He rushed to its aid and gently picked it up cupping his hands. He swiftly turned around and called out to us to show off his treasure.

"Look at this little birdie," he said. "It flew a long way to get here, and now it may not survive. It needs help."

He gaped tenderly at the swallow, as if it was the most precious thing in the world. Nothing else mattered to him anymore. I was close enough to feel George's breath. That thought gave me goose bumps.

Our new feathered friend was so scared. It tried to break out of his palms a few times but could not escape. Not knowing what to do someone inquired if he could take it home to feed it. No time for that. We couldn't leave the place until the shoot was done. Scrambling for a solution, I just stood there, watching powerless the little bird's struggle.

The girls in the choir admired George. They sang to be noticed. A story went around that he asked one of the lead sopranos to marry him a few years ago but she turned him down. Others said he was gay. So, we teased him whenever we had a chance. He teased us back by calling us funny names and picking on us. It was all a game. We had lots of fun.

Suddenly an unmistakable sound of a snapping camera caught my attention. I looked around but couldn't see anything special.

"Did you hear that?" I double checked it with George.

"Hear what?" he asked in return.

"I am not sure. I thought I heard a camera snapping photos. It came from that bush there," I said, pointing it out to him.

"Don't worry about it. It's probably nothing. The shoot is about to begin, get ready" he muttered, examining the swallow carefully. "It's frozen, poor thing." And he started blowing gently his warm breath into the cupped hands, as he was climbing down the hill.

Something moved again near the same crest as before and this time I clearly heard the familiar snap. My heart was pounding. Is anyone watching us? Why would they do that? I decided to call for George.

He was chatting with some other fellows down below and didn't hear me. Then, he turned around, raised his arms up in the air, still holding the swallow, and signalled us to start the rehearsal.

The music was loud. Two huge speakers were blasting from the walkway. We clutched our hands and started spinning slowly on the grass, round, and round, in two concentrical circles, stretching our arms in and out, in a traditional Romanian folklore dance called "Hora." We kept spinning faster and faster following the music in a frenzy. As we lost control we eventually stumbled in the grass, laughing, until we were asked to stop.

During the first break I sneaked out to the bush to suss out the hiding place: a middle-aged male, in a black shirt, black tie, black leather coat and dark sunglasses was watching us. "State Security Services," I thought. "Ouch!" Camera in his left hand pointed at George was taking photos in a rush. Worried, I waved at George urging for his attention. He missed it.

Someone from the production team called him to give more instructions, so he signalled us to continue without him.

I was feeling increasingly anxious. Normally he would have been with us the whole time, leading the way. This time he didn't.

Not far from us the woman with the pram was viewing the spectacle unfolding.

We began rehearsing again without George. He positioned himself behind the cameraman filming us and continued to breathe into his cupped hands, but at the same time, kept directing us following his own ideas, despite the disapprovals and threats babbled by the TV directors on site. We followed only his advice. He had trained us well. One gesture from him was all we needed, like an encrypted code, and everything worked out perfectly on screen.

The girls admired his charisma, wittiness, and good looks; the boys revered his courage and talent. We all loved his abilities to achieve success in the challenging local musical environment, both on stage and on TV, at a time when success was tightly monitored and could even be synonym to danger. He made us feel important as human beings, as individuals. We felt creative and alive around him.

Even if the propaganda directors grumbled and disparaged him, unwilling to accept his defiant working style, they all admitted at the end of the day that he was the best. He knew what he was doing and had great artistic skills.

Second break was announced. I sprinted downhill and accidently stumbled, straining my knee. A camera snapped behind me. That doesn't sound good, I thought, and continued my journey limping downhill.

I had to warn George. He'd know what to do.

"What's wrong?" He asked when I reached him.

I murmured in his ear my encounter with the man in black. Without a word, George turned around and headed straight up to the hiding place. The TV directors tried to stop him, but he ignored them. When he reached the bush, he asked the intruder in a loud but firm voice to show himself. Everyone on site went completely quiet. The music paused too. However, the man in black didn't move.

"If you don't come out at once, I'll pull you out myself and take your camera as well," George threatened. Still nothing.

A few icy moments passed until the man in black decided to step out in the open. George measured him up for a moment and confronted him in a low tone pointing to his camera. The conversation seemed strained. Two men flexing their power in a tensed standoff. I could not hear an iota.

Everybody on the set was wondering what was going to happen. Will George be arrested? We all knew what State Security Services were capable of, so nobody dared to say anything. Opposing the regime was not an option at any point in time. You could disappear overnight never to be seen again if they thought you were a danger to their policies.

After about five minutes the argument ended. The man in black with a grim face pointing the finger at George left the scene. George remained calm, still holding his swallow in his hands, and returned to us with a smile. We surrounded him curious to hear what happened. He shook his head. "Nothing happened... Are you going to finish the shoot today or what?" he added and asked the TV directors for a final run.

We were intrigued but followed his instructions. I was so worried but kept it to myself.

The shoot in the park came to an end.

It was then when George opened up to me. He was considered suspicious by the State Security Services. Over the years they had brought up some serious allegations against him to keep him in line.

"I am really concerned about you" I blurted.

He shrugged. "Don't be." His dark brown eyes sparkled. "They have a file on all of us, that's what they do."

He blew one more warm breath over his hands and winked at me. "Don't worry about them!" a twinkle in his eye. My heart fluttered involuntarily.

At this point I noticed the woman with the pram talking to the man in black. "Really? Was she in it too?" I wondered. He slipped his camera into the pram, and together they strolled away.

We were about to leave the scene when the swallow started to flap its wings, visibly perking up a little. George's keen eye caught sight of a sheltered spot bathed in the warmth of the mid-day sun. He lowered himself into a squatting position until his clasped hands contacted the ground. He slowly unfurled his palms and waited... The swallow raised its head cautiously, stretched its delicate feet, took a moment to contemplate, and prudently stepped out of the impromptu cage. It took a few steps, testing its newfound strength, paused to shake its head, spread its wings, straightened its body, and soared towards a nearby branch.

I held my breath witnessing its venture into a new life. It found a temporary respite in the sunlight before taking flight once more. It circled the tree a couple of times, swooping closely to George, who watched in awe, and flew away.

As I traced its path through the sky, a pledge took hold of my heart: "Fly away, little bird", I whispered, "my time will come". I knew then and there it was only a matter of time.

There is a First for Everything

A teenager navigates her new adopted country and embraces the new culture.

Angela was engrossed in her favourite mystery novel when she received the invite for the Melbourne Cup event at a local pub in Ramsgate, a southern Sydney suburb. She had lived in Australia for only six months, and she had never heard of it. The call was from Brian. They had met a few weeks back, as his younger brother was in the same class as her. Brian was nineteen and had graduated from the same high school as Angela the previous year. He was at that stage of figuring out what he wanted to do with his life. Right now, he was working part-time at the Sunset restaurant in the city.

"What is this about?" Angela asked.

"What do you mean? Haven't you heard about the famous Melbourne Cup race day? People in Melbourne have a Public Holiday for Melbourne Cup!" Brian replied in disdain.

"Sorry, I had no idea. And I have never been a race fan anyway. So, thank you, but I'll pass." Angela concluded.

"No, no, you have to come and see for yourself. It's a must. Haven't you said that you wanted to learn more about us Aussies?" Brian pressed.

"Yes, but..."

"No buts. This is a special event, please come!" he pleaded.

"My father wouldn't agree to this," she thought, but she enquired, "What's the dress code?" "Oh, you have to wear a hat!" he stated.

"Do you mean a funny hat?" the girl asked.

"No, I mean a fashionable hat, one that a lady would wear," Brian said. "They give prizes for the most stylish ones, you know."

"Oh, God," she thought, "Hats are not my thing. And my father wouldn't like the idea anyway."

"I'll buy one for you if you want me to," Brian added.

"No, no, I'll work it out, but thanks for the offer," said Angela.

"How can I tell my father that I'm going out with this guy to a party?" Angela wondered.

She stopped worrying when she hung up. She had a whole week to figure it out until the Melbourne Cup gathering on Tuesday and she was intrigued. Being an immigrant from Cologne, Germany, Angela hasn't heard of horse-racing during her school years back home. And the fact that her dad was so strict about her going out with boys he didn't know would not make this outing any easier.

Angela had moved to Australia with her parents. She was eighteen, tall and slender, with intelligent green eyes. Because of that big move, she had lost one school year, but she wasn't concerned about that. It was hard enough to work on her English as a second language every day, and to make new friends in a completely new country that celebrated Christmas in the middle of summer!! She didn't want her parents to know that she had her fair share of tears every now and then. Being an immigrant was difficult, especially when her mother, Brigitte, had her own personal struggles and financial worries to deal with.

Luckily enough, her father, Robert, an experienced aviation engineer, had been offered a wonderful opportunity in his company, a major airline, to run the aircraft maintenance area. Angela loved her father very much. She looked up to him. When she was a child, he used to take her in his arms and throw her up high to touch the ceiling with her little palms in their family home, catching her back just before reaching the floor. What a thrill. It was their game, their bonding time. Once she grew into a teenager though, things changed. She felt she was no longer his "little girl". He was working hard all the time. He was not there like before. And then this move to the other side of the planet made things even more challenging. Talking to him became complicated.

Angela was swamped with homework during the week and completely forgot about Brian's invite. Time flew by. Everyone was busy. Angela's mother was cooking and looking after the house. Her father was either working or sneaking off to the pub for a beer with his new work mates. On Monday morning Angela could not postpone it anymore and asked her mother nicely if she could go to the races with Brian. Brigitte approved. "Aww! That was easy, what a relief." Angela sighed. They agreed not to tell her father about it for now.

Better not risk it. He would be at work anyway by the time Angela came back from the pub.

Mother and daughter set off for Miranda shopping centre to look for a fancy hat and a nice dress. But the prices! Their enthusiasm diminished quickly. It was clear they could not afford both. Her father would never approve of the expense, especially now that he was the only breadwinner. "Too late to cancel Brian's invite now," Angela thought, but she didn't want to let him think she couldn't pull it off. Perhaps she should just claim she had a migraine. Her mother had other plans. She led Angela into a store and bought some red shiny fabric, threads, a headband, and a red mesh. At home she cut the material into these rose petal shapes, sewing them together up top carefully.

"What's going on here?" Robert asked when he arrived home that night.

"You are late!" Brigitte replied in return. "Your dinner is in the oven."

Rob took his work jacket off and wobbled through the kitchen, looking for a clear pathway. He sat down and ate quietly and then went straight to bed.

"Good night, ladies" he said, bouncing up the stairs.

When Brigitte and Angela finished the outfit, it was almost four o'clock in the morning. Finally, they stitched the last bit of lace at the back. The hat was just a bit bigger than Angela's palm. It looked elegant and set off Angela's light brown curls. She suppressed a big yawn and fell asleep on the couch. By the time Brigitte cleaned up the mess, the first sunrays were creeping through the blinds.

Brian was supposed to pick up Angela at ten o'clock and drive to the local pub, about five kilometres away. At nine sharp, Angela was showering, eyes still encrusted from lack of sleep. She hadn't heard Rob leaving for work that morning and she still couldn't believe she was going out for the first time on her own since living in Australia. She looked in the mirror and sobbed. Huge eye bags. Oh well, it was not like she was meeting with her sweetheart. She didn't have one.

Brian was just a friend as far as she was concerned. Deep down she hoped she would meet someone hot one day, hopefully soon, even if she didn't really know what "hot" exactly meant. She'd know it when the time came.

Her mother knocked at the bathroom door.

"Come on darling, while we are still young!" she hurried her daughter. Angela took another glance in the mirror and pulled some faces. "When I have my own place, I will not allow anyone to rush me out like that," she thought and finished rolling her curly hair. She glimpsed outside and saw Brian standing at the front gate. "Great, he's already here," she exclaimed and hurried herself.

"Mum, what if Dad finds out about this?" Angela asked, rushing to her room.

"Let me worry about that, my darling. Now, get yourself out of here and have some fun!" her mother replied, preparing to go to the fruit market. Angela's red silky dress embraced her bust and curved down on her young hips. It was a great fit. Now for the hat. The pièce de résistance. Angela set it on an angle, on the left. She had seen it in a movie, you place it on your head, anchor it with a few invisible hairpins, and you smile seductively from down-up, flipping your eyelashes. She rehearsed for a minute, swivelled on her high heels, to exercise her balance, grabbed her little beige satin purse and strutted confidently out.

Brian was having a cigarette. When he saw Angela, a "Wow! You look amazing!" slipped from his mouth.

"Thank you," said Angela, feeling a bit embarrassed by his remark, but especially his look. The eternal look of a young man meeting a beautiful woman.

"He's such a peasant!" she thought. "He could have at least tried to cover that pervy look in his eyes."

It took him a couple more seconds to recompose his drooling, and off they went to the race party. Together they entered the already-packed pub. Brian kept his eyes out for his mates. He wanted them to see him with Angela. He felt so proud. She was a stunner. When

Angela stepped in, she literally turned heads. She was clearly new to the surroundings, and people noticed her.

The place was full of all kinds of fellows, from locals to guests from overseas. The elegant ladies were looking terribly busy with their newspapers and betting cards in their hands. Fascinators scattered everywhere.

"I guess it was worth the effort, sewing mine last night," Angela giggled to herself. Brian's aunt Wilma was sitting at the centre table. She looked smart in a light sandy dress outlining her great figure, with a decent V cut, adorned with some beautiful Majorca pearls and a chic hat to go with her necklace. Her eyes were sparkling with curiosity.

"Angela, please meet my aunt Wilma," Brian said. Then he looked around and walked away. Angela wanted to say something, but no words came out in the confusion. Wilma invited her to sit down near her and showed her the race cards.

"Who is your money on?" she asked Angela kindly.

"I'd bet, if I knew how," Angela finally recomposed herself. The aunt gently explained how the betting worked.

It was still fifteen minutes until the first race started. Angela picked up the newspaper and looked at the horses' names. Then she had a glimpse at their odds but could not understand a thing, so she dismissed them. She started marking her choices, as if she knew what she was doing. She picked a horse for the first race, then noted down selected horses for each race throughout the day without thinking. Gut feeling entirely. She put two dollars "each way" to keep it simple, four dollars in total. She only had thirty dollars to play with, and that was a stretch.

On the way to the cashier, Wilma asked her what horses she had picked and checked them against her own list.

"Hmmm...Yours are completely different from mine," Wilma noticed, "Are you sure you don't want to learn more about the horses before you make your final decision?"

"It's OK, thank you" Angela replied "I'll go with what I picked". While pondering her options in her mind, she thought she heard a familiar voice and turned to the left but saw no one special.

"Off we go and place them then," Wilma said, "Quickly, they are about to close the bets for the first race!"

They just made it in time.

After a couple of minutes, the first race started. Some people in the room were standing, others sitting. Everybody was watching the big TV screens hung up high on the walls. Brian offered Wilma and Angela drinks, champagne for Wilma and a soft drink for Angela, as requested, and then he went away again, to his beer buddies. This time Angela didn't mind seeing him leaving, but she was a bit intrigued by his behaviour. This was supposed to be like a date she thought, their standards were obviously different. She watched the first horse race ever, trying to see where her horse was located during the competition. By the time it ended, she couldn't even tell which the top three winners were. So many colours and the whole thing went so fast. Very confusing. Wilma checked her cards and nodded her head. "One-off!" she said and scrunched up her card. "Yours came third. Well done, Angela!"

"I picked a winner!" Angela thought and smiled angelically. The next race was in an hour.

Everyone was chatting away about their own winnings and losses, sipping champagne, beer, or soft drinks. The two ladies accompanying Wilma came by, and Wilma mentioned Angela's first winning.

"That was Angela's first horse race ever in her life. Isn't that great? Let me introduce you, darling, to my dear old friends, Betty, and Thelma," she said, turning towards Angela.

"Nice to meet you" Angela replied.

"And now ladies, let's celebrate!" said Wilma raising her glass.

By this time, the pub was crowded. The men were surrounding the bar and the two pool tables. The women were sitting at the tables, having a good laugh. At times, they mingled. Angela was watching the people around the room, talking, and enjoying each other's company, and concluded they were quite a friendly and welcoming bunch, nothing to worry about. Being for the first time away on her own in Australia, she felt at ease.

The second race was about to start. All eyes glued to the TVs once again, voices shouting in support of their favourites. This race was tough, horses were running shoulder to shoulder. At the finish line, the winner wasn't clear. They needed a split picture to confirm the finalist. People were anxious to find out the champion. With beer glasses in their hands, the men were debating the finish line, waiting for the decision.

When it was finally announced, blood invaded Angela's cheeks. She had a second-place winner. Wilma and her friends didn't win anything again, but they were happy to celebrate Angela's success. They chin-chined and asked Angela about her third pick. After a quick thought, the three of them decided to bet some ten dollars on Apollo, Angela's next horse in line.

Brian came along and congratulated Angela. She was excited. She told him she had decided to get rid of all her worries and make the most of this wonderful day. Brian laughed "That's the spirit".

"Nice bum, I give him that," she concluded while following his silhouette on his way back to his friends. She noticed three young men in his group, whom she didn't think much of, and some older individuals, one of whom was wearing a soccer cap and a green T-shirt. She couldn't see his face from where she was standing, but his broad shoulders reminded her of someone she thought she knew. "Next time, I'll ask Brian who that was," she promised herself.

By the time the third race finished, Angela had learned much more about the Melbourne Cup event. In between the races, they were showing images of the actual Melbourne Cup racing place on screen. She was impressed: all the ladies so nicely dressed, like for a fashion parade, their hats sticking out, the whole grounds packed with people cheering and having fun. Everything was so vibrant, including the jockeys. And the horses looked incredible too. Angela fell in love with them, as they were introduced to the public one by one.

Back in the south Sydney pub, Angela was checking her winnings. She had won second place in the third race. Woo-hoo! The ladies around her looked somewhat surprised. Who is this strange young lady winning the day? A few men came along and congratulated her as well. Angela enjoyed their enthusiasm. At this point, Brian was so excited by her success that he kissed her on the cheek. She blushed.

After lunch, the Melbourne Cup race was announced that it would start in a few minutes. Everybody was talking louder and louder, bursting into laughter here and there, waiting for the signal. The adrenaline rush reached its peak. When the horse race started, the crowd hit the highest thrill, almost in unison, men and women spitting their guts out, shouting and gesticulating, pointing at their favourite horses. Angela held her breath. Her heart was racing along with the horses, her hands clenched together in a nervous frenzy. Ah! This time she lost. None of her two picks made it up to the top three.

She suddenly felt sad. Now that the Cup ended, she wanted more. It finished so quickly. People wait for a whole year to watch this exhilarating show, and it all ends in just a few minutes. "Not fair," she thought. Everybody went back to their places and the noise toned down for a while.

Brian came along and enquired about her next move. "That's strange," she thought. "He hasn't asked me before about any of my choices." She told him she would bet more this time, on a whim, in the final round. She mentioned her pick and asked him about his.

"I haven't decided yet," he said, "but thanks for the tip." He smiled and disappeared into the crowd once again.

"Hey, wait!" she remembered, "I want to ask you something."

"Not now, Angela, we need to place the bets." The next race was scheduled to begin soon. "One final bet," she figured, and discreetly counted the cash she had won "Sixty dollars, not bad. I doubled my thirty, even with the outlay on bets and drinks for the day." she concluded.

"What the hell," she thought, "I'll have a splurge on this last race, and bet ten dollars 'each way'. " She selected the horse.

"This Anenkov must be the winner!" she exclaimed, drawing Wilma's attention.

"Do you really think so dear? It's at one hundred to one odds!"

Not really understanding what Wilma was talking about, she placed her bet. To her, the name felt lucky. Then she looked for Brian, hoping he would give her a lift back home as soon as the race had finished. Brian was nowhere to be found. She could see his drinking mates in the same spot, but he wasn't there. Nor was the man with the soccer cap. "Where the hell is he when you need him?" she wondered, bouncing on her legs.

The last race of the day finally started. People were quiet at this stage, few had hardly placed any bets, though all eyes were staring at the television screens. Angela watched the race anxiously. At the first corner, her horse was in the lead, at the start of the straight run he was three lengths at the head of the field. As Anenkov approached the finish line, he was six lengths clear of the nearest horse behind him. Angela found herself screaming eagerly "Run, Run, Run!"

"And the winner is Anenkov", the TV speaker blasted. All eyes turned to Angela, who was still in a state of disbelief, yelling uncontrollably "I won, I won, I won!" It was one of the happiest moments she could remember in recent years. After a few minutes, the payout figures appeared on the TV screens.

"Oh my God," stuttered Wilma, hardly believing what she was reading. She turned to Angela and blurted, "Angela dear, that's over a thousand dollars you've won!"

Angela whooped and jumped for joy, knowing this would be a happy return home. She could take some financial pressure off her parents now, at least for a short time. Betty and Thelma hugged Angela repeatedly. People congratulated her over and over. Brian sneaked behind her and grabbed her shoulders in a friendly hug.

"Where were you?" she asked him inquisitively. He ran away again without an answer. "What a scumbag!" she thought. This time she was annoyed.

She picked up her things really annoyed and straightened her dress. Wilma came to say goodbye, and whispered in her ear, "There is a first time for everything my dear." Without paying much attention to her words, Angela delivered her polite goodbyes and rushed to the exit door. She had no idea how she was going to get back home.

"Angela, wait!" she heard a familiar voice behind her.

"Dad?" Her face turned pale, and her body cringed, while staring at him.

"Don't worry Angela. It's all good. I came here with my workmates. When I saw you winning, you were so happy, I didn't want to spoil your day." he explained.

"Dad, I am really sorry I didn't tell you about this!" she exclaimed, tears rolling down her face. "Shush... Come on, let's get you home!" Rob gave her a big loving hug, and she felt like his "little girl" once again.

When they were about to leave, Brian appeared out of nowhere. He stood there, trying to gauge Angela's reaction, his arms hanging hopelessly, his body tense.

"Thank you, Brian," Rob took the initiative and shook his hand. "I asked Brian not to tell you I was here," he said to Angela. She raised her head, wiped her face with her palms, fixed her hair, steadied her hat, and finally gave Brian a quick "I'm not done with you yet" look.

Then the father and daughter exited the pub.

"You know my dear," her father said casually on their way to the car, offering her his arm affectionately, "On the last pick, I placed a hundred dollars 'each way' on your horse. You did so well. I'm very proud of you." Angela's brain started crunching frantically the numbers, while her mind kept echoing Wilma's last words: "There is a first for everything."

Unmasking the Truth

Lies, corruption and intrigue, but in the end the truth wins.

He was tired that early Friday morning, when he landed in Sydney airport. He had had a rough week with a lot of business meetings in Paris and its surroundings. Nobody wanted to buy anything, despite his best efforts. That dreadful "Au revoir, Monsieur!" was persisting in his ears, while he passed through customs. He had enough of this running around, trying to sell people these bloody IT systems that nobody was interested in, or so they said. Until they reached a decision, he had to pull all the tricks he could think of. Especially in France, he found French people difficult to work with and their funny accents difficult to understand.

He felt relieved every time he was coming back home, where he could relax for a couple of days, go to the gym, meet some old buddies downtown for a drink and then get ready to start all over again.

Thomas was a talented sale rep, working for a London-based software company. He was tall, shaved bald, had dark blue eyes and a square masculine face, plus a fit body. Women loved him. At 37 years old, all that travelling around the world, that gave an initial advantage in front of his friends, had long lost its glamour and he had started to feel tired of it. Every time he was going out with his mates back home in Sydney, he could read their envy in their eyes. They all thought he had the best life anyone could possibly ask for, flying to London, Paris, Madrid, Vienna, and the rest, almost every month. But Thomas learnt otherwise. He was literally living out of a suitcase for the last ten years of his life and he had enough. "Personal life, what personal life?" he wondered bitterly. Who would want to date a person who lives in a perpetual jet-lagged state?

"Get a life" Thomas said to himself, sitting in the service bus, staring at the window, on his way back to the Long-Term Parking Lot in Sydney Airport. He tried to remember where he had parked his car a week ago, when luckily, he found his ticket just in time to get off the vehicle at the correct parking station.

"It needs a wash" he mumbled when he approached his black Toyota Pajero. He liked his car. He had bought it three years ago, brand new, from a local car dealer, not far from where he lived, and it has served him well. He enjoyed taking care of his car when he was home.

So, he threw his suitcase in the rear, opened the driver's side door, climbed behind the wheel, and turned on the engine. After adjusting his seat belt, turned on his indicator, checked his right and moved out of the parking space.

He navigated the car around the meandering laneways towards the exit of the short-term car park. As he neared the exit pay booths, a light grey Mercedes convertible stormed out of nowhere, from an up ramp, going down the ramp, cutting him off. "What the hell!" he cried while instinctively jamming the brakes, only to avoid collision by an inch.

The Mercedes stopped in front of him, blocking his way out. He cut his engine off and took a deep breath while opening his window. The stench of burning rubber was thick in the air, as he attempted to identify the occupant of the Mercedes. Through the dark-tinted windows, he couldn't see a thing. The front passenger window rolled down slightly, still giving him no clear indication of the driver.

"What are you doing? You almost crashed into my car" he said peering into the gap in the passenger side of the Mercedes.

"Go to hell, idiot!" a harsh alto voice blasted out of the grey car.

"Excuse me?" Thomas asked in utter amazement. "YOU cut me off, lady! You didn't even look. And you went the wrong way down the ramp, do you have any idea how dangerous that is?" he added, still trying to see who he was talking to.

"Oh yeah! Well look at this, moron," and she flipped him the bird. Thomas was stunned, having never witnessed such unladylike behaviour, he was lost for words. He heard a noise emit from the other car's interior that he could not place, as the window fully opened and caught a glimpse of the female driver. "Back off, you fool!" she snarled and slammed the car into gear and accelerated away.

Before he knew it, he was left choking on a combination of car exhaust and tyre smoke.

"Bloody hell" he shrugged and clenched his fists. "What a cow!"

He turned on the engine and drove home furiously, constantly checking his rear windows. Something didn't feel quite right. When he finally got to his apartment, pushed his suitcase away from his doorstep, unleashed his tie, scampered his socks and undies on his way to the bathroom and jumped in the shower. The hot water calmed him down a bit.

That woman's face, a trendy-looking middle-aged blonde, triggered a memory from his childhood, of that sinister character, Cruella de Vil, from the 101 Dalmatians cartoon story. "All she was missing was the fur stole and the long cigarette, otherwise she looked exactly like her; even her voice sounded chillingly similar," he thought, thrilled by her resemblance. Her evil eyes with their long eyelashes still lingered on his mind for a while.

"What a day!" he thought, plunging in a deep night's sleep.

The next morning, he got up early and went to the gym. He was feeling stiff, and his body was screaming for some physical, especially after such a long journey like Paris. He started his exercise circuit at seven, worked through the different stations, and finished with the punching bag. He loved the punching bag. It helped him lay some steam off, especially when he was angry at someone.

When he reached the office at nine o'clock, everybody was busy looking for a cup of coffee. The coffee machine had broken down and they were all complaining to a young trainee assistant, who had worked overtime during the weekend, accusing her of crashing it. When she couldn't take the pressure anymore, the girl ran to the bathroom and locked herself in. Everybody went back to their places and forgot about the event in no time, like it never happened.

"Morning" Thomas said, passing the reception desk.

"Morning. How are you?" asked Clara, the secretary, smiling at him, while scanning some papers. "How was Paris?"

"Boring", he replied.

Clara nodded her head and added "Your Tokyo report of two weeks ago is on your desk. Boss wants to have its final version by noon today" she asked, while picking up a call.

"Like I care..." he whispered to himself on his way to the coffee point.

Luckily enough, the boss wasn't around that morning, so Thomas decided to have a look at some statistics first and got completely absorbed in his work.

At eleven fifteen Clara called and asked him to pick up line 3. The police wanted to talk to him. He answered the phone reluctantly, still thinking of his report, convinced that the call was not for him, but he took it anyway.

"Is this Mr Thomas Adams?" a male voice asked over the phone.

"Speaking. How can I help you?" Thomas answered automatically.

"My name is Detective Senior Constable John Hudson, from Mascot Police station. Are you the owner of a black Toyota Pajero, license plate number OPO99K?" asked Hudson.

"Yes, what appears to be the problem? Has something happened to my car?" Thomas replied, starting to feel slightly anxious.

"Well, there was an incident that we would like to discuss with you about. Do you think you could come down to the station immediately?" requested Hudson.

"Sure, no problem!" Thomas continued. "Could you please give me an idea about what the problem is?"

"I can assure you, sir, that all will be revealed when you arrive. Just ask for DSC Hudson at reception." and he hung up.

Thomas was confused. His mind went frantically looking for a reason of why the Police would want to see him, and at such a short notice. "Maybe it's related to a speed ticket?" he figured, scratching his head.

When he arrived at Mascot Police station, DS Constable Hudson was waiting for him. He shook his hand and invited him into an interview room and offered him a seat. Then he told Thomas that there was a complaint filed against him, by which he has been accused of assaulting a lady in a public place, specifically in the Sydney Airport area, the previous day. Thomas's jaw dropped in disbelief. He was stunned.

"Assault?" he shouted in disdain. The DS Constable nodded in an official manner.

"You've got to be kidding me!" Thomas exclaimed bitterly. "This is the biggest lie I've ever heard! Who is this woman anyway?" Thomas articulated.

"The lady's name is Helen O'Hara." Then he paused as if he wasn't sure if to continue or not. Eventually he added in a low voice "She is our Police Commissioner's sister-in-law, her husband's a barrister working in one of the top chambers in Sydney." he noted with a touch of sympathy.

A bewildered Adams, blinked twice to ensure he wasn't dreaming, but the nightmare continued, as he protested his innocence to DS Constable Hudson.

"Sorry, sir, we need to take a formal statement during the interview. The lady in question has made a criminal complaint, and you will be charged with assault." he stated and left the room.

Thomas sat down and hid his face in his cupped hands. His head was spinning. "I'm in real deep trouble here" he thought.

The interviewing officer informed him that the interview would be taped, and he would be furnished with a copy. He gave Thomas a questioning look, who nodded back in the affirmative, that he understood what was happening. After they completed the interview, Thomas was formally charged with assault, fingerprinted, and released on his own recognisance. The departing comments of the DS Constable entrenched firmly in his mind. "Get yourself a good solicitor!" he said in a sympathetic manner that suggested he didn't like the situation any more than the alleged offender.

Thomas scorched his memory and at some point, he remembered he had a long-forgotten friend from his high school days, Paul Carter, who had turned into a successful solicitor, or so he had heard. "Top priority. Get on to Paul. Fast!" he commanded himself, on his way back to the office.

After securing the services of his "not-so-cheap" former friend, Paul, Thomas was able to openly discuss his matter with him for hours, as Paul had found out some interesting facts about the case while preparing for his defence.

In the end, Paul turned to Thomas, leaned his back against the luxurious office desk, crossed his arms, and asked him in a deadpan voice, with a steel look in his eyes "Did you hit her?"

The look of panic spread across Thomas's face "Of course not. She was so rude and angry towards me, but I never left my car! So, if I never left my car, how could I have hit her?" he rationally explained.

Paul turned around without a word, walked towards his office balcony and lit a cigarette, deep in thought. The meeting was over.

Thomas returned to his apartment and fixed himself a large whiskey. "Did Paul believe me?" he wondered, looking up through the bedroom window at the stars, and had another sip.

When he received the court notice, after two weeks, he got worried. His appearance was set for a Monday morning, three weeks from then. Time dragged away.

On the day of the trial, Thomas arrived at court, half an hour early. He was a complete wreck. He hasn't been able to eat or sleep lately, even though he took sleeping pills. Only thinking of that woman made his stomach tumble.

When he was called in, he was wound up already.

First, he was asked to tell his version of what had happened that day at the airport, which he did. When Mrs O'Hara turned up, he could hardly stop himself from heading to her neck. Helen O'Hara walked stiffly to the stand and took the floor in a powerful voice. According to her, Thomas had jumped out of his car and pulled her out of hers, with his bare hands, hurting her neck. To prove that she presented the court with a set of photographs, which showed her badly bruised neck and arms in detail. She claimed she had got them from his clenched fingers when she opposed him. Additionally, she reported he would have slapped her face repeatedly in anger. Finally, she told the court that he had pushed her back, against her car, causing her serious damage to her lower back. To top it up, she provided a medical certificate from her doctor stating her bruises condition at the time.

Thomas was speechless.

After a few moments, the Magistrate called for a half an hour recess and left the room.

People raised and poured out the court's open doors. So did Paul and Thomas. They lit their cigarettes without looking at each other while sitting down on the steps close to the main entrance.

"Those photos are enough to convict me" Thomas realised in a loud voice and turned to Paul. "Damn it, I wish there was somebody around that day to prove my innocence." he cried.

Paul asked Thomas to be patient, as he had identified a new lead. Before he had a chance to explain what he was talking about, they got asked to go back in.

When the court returned, Paul called this person, Peter Clark, to take the stand, as a witness of that day's event. Thomas was perplexed. He has never heard of him.

When Mr Clark stepped into the courtroom and walked down the rows, all eyes followed him with great interest. "Who the hell is this guy?" Thomas wondered, staring at his face.

Paul gave a sly smile and winked at Tom before turning to the court to address this mystery witness. After a deep breath Paul said:" Please state your name and occupation for the court."

"Peter Clark, and I am a security and surveillance consultant." He smiled slightly back at Paul and continued. "Some would say I'm a Private Investigator."

Then Paul invited Mr Clark to tell the court his story.

He started in a confident tone, while everybody kept quiet.

"On the day of the incident in question, I was sitting in my car, in the airport carpark, on the ground level, quite near the exit gates, about 20 meters away from the junction where Mrs O'Hara encountered Mr Adams. From my location, I had a clear view of everything that happened in the street."

After a short pause, he continued.

"There was no assault whatsoever that day. That is a lie" and he scrutinised the room towards Mrs O'Hara's direction. Her eyes fired poison at him in return.

"It was Mrs O'Hara who caused the altercation and called Mr Adams an idiot and flipped her middle finger at him. She never left her car; neither did he. So, he could not have possibly been able to touch her at all, at any time."

"Yes, thank God!" Thomas sighed in relief.

Paul continued to question the witness about his reason for being in the hotel parking lot that day.

"I was following a suspect" he replied imperturbably.

"Is that suspect in this room?" the solicitor continued.

"Yes" the investigator confirmed.

"Would you identify the suspect for the court please?" Paul persisted.

"The suspect was Mrs O'Hara, who is sitting right there" he answered, pointing at her, and masking a malicious smile with a cough.

"And why were you following Mrs O'Hara that day, Mr Clark?" Paul insisted.

"Objection" the prosecutor intervened.

"I'm afraid I am not at liberty to disclose that, sir" Peter refused to answer politely.

"Then let me ask you something else. Is it possible, that Mrs O'Hara's bruises might have been inflicted prior to the moment of her encounter with Mr Adam in the street that day?" Paul followed a hunch.

"More than plausible, I would say" the investigator affirmed.

"And would you have any knowledge about how those bruises had been inflicted on Mrs O'Hara?" the solicitor continued.

"Objection" the prosecutor interjected again.

The Magistrate turned to Mr Clark and explained to him that, starting from that moment, he would have to disclose to the court everything he knew about Mrs O Hara's wounds.

Peter Clark took a deep breath, gathered his thoughts, and began to present the facts.

Everyone in the court room held their breath.

"Mrs O'Hara was having an affair with a man in the Hilton Hotel that morning, and things got violent. The man she was having the affair with was a sex offender, known by the Police for over ten years. His Modum Operandi was having sex with married women in high places and then threatened them with exposing their affair if they didn't pay up. He would use violence towards them to extort money if they didn't conform to his demands. Mrs O'Hara was lucky to get out without a more severe injury. These are the pictures I've taken, as evidence to supplement my statement" he concluded and offered a big envelope to the bailiff.

"Oh my God" Thomas thought, "Lucky me to get in her way that day!"

"You may step down, Mr Clark" the Magistrate released him.

The trial finished quickly after that. Charges were dropped. The case was closed.

Thomas was congratulated profusely, and so was Paul. TV cameras appeared at the court's main entrance, and a news reporter approached Mrs O'Hara, asking her about her violent love affairs. "No comment" she shouted and pushed him away, barely making her way ahead through the crowd.

Thomas sneaked behind some students, near one of the lateral entrance doors and lit another cigarette. He inhaled the nicotine hungrily then released it slowly, making circles. Through the swirls he noticed Peter Clark marching to the parking lot.

Thomas sprinted to a shortcut and called him, throwing his cigarette away. Peter stopped and waited for him.

"I would like to thank you, Mr Clark" said Thomas, catching his breath "and to shake your hand."

Peter looked at him. "You may call me Peter" he replied and shook Thomas's hand.

"Peter, may I ask you one more question, please?" Thomas tried his luck.

"Go ahead." Peter agreed.

"I was just wondering." Thomas continued doubtfully. "What made you come through to tell the truth about what really happened that day? After all, nobody knew you were there and your statement in court today might cost you your job. I am sure you are aware that Mrs O'Hara's brother-in-law is the Police Commissioner in Sydney."

Peter smiled at him and added "When her barrister husband found out about his wife's affair with that lowlife, he wouldn't pay me a zack. Moreover, he threatened me with his police high ranking brother that he would come after me and cancel my private investigator's license, as I knew too much about their dodgy deals. Husband and wife are as bad as each other. I figured, at least I should give them a reason" and he slowly walked away to his car.

Close Call in Bondi

Courage and quick thinking can make all the difference.

I am driving home from work on a gloomy rainy Friday evening. So glad the week is over so I can spend some time on my own.

I'm 35, single and have an awesome job in PR in the city, which pays for my bills and rent of my new little apartment in Bondi. I feel good and am contemplating my options for this weekend. Should I go out or stay in tonight?

It's peak hour and the traffic is jammed. My mind is thinking over that last meeting at work that felt like it would never end.

Suddenly this alerted voice on the radio catches my attention "...the convict has miraculously escaped from Long Bay prison last night around 20.00 hours and is at large. The Police statement will follow shortly." What the hell is going on? I just moved to the Eastern Suburbs. I was told it is quite a good area to live in. I switch on the radio to a different channel and hope to hear some more info on the subject and automatically press the car lock button.

By the time I park my car, it is already dark. Finally at home. I get my bag and the red rose I received today and rush to the elevator, looking carefully around me. Nobody in site and the elevator is empty. Good. I jump in and press the second-floor button. I can hear my heart pumping on the way up. Almost there.

Finally, I'm inside. I feel safe. Lights on and my anguish disappears. My tablet resting on the armchair sounds like a good idea to turn on and listen to some old Temptations soundtrack for a couple of minutes. Love it. I rest my handbag on the dresser and look for a vase and some water to save the beautiful red rose in my hand and place it as a centrepiece on the dining table. It smells so nice. I stop for a moment to breathe in its fragrance. Now, a shower and I'm all set for the evening.

I like my new place even if you find yourself in the middle of it in only five steps from the entrance door. My bed along the left wall faces the window. It's nice to feel the sunshine on my face in the morning before I open my eyes. On the right-hand side my shoes are lined up on three levels, like soldiers' flanks before battle. The wardrobe hangs out freely from the ceiling, with all its compartments filled to their limits. Colour coding to follow. And there is more stuff to come, I figure. Hold that thought for another day.

Let me watch some TV and have a nice dinner. Breaking news pops up on the TV screen. Oh, no, not again.

"A convict is at large in Sydney tonight. Anyone who sees or hears anything suspicious please call immediately the police numbers displayed below."

My heart starts racing again. Out of nowhere, I'm having a flashback to when I was five. My father, a police commander, in his shiny uniform in front of my bedroom mirror, was teaching me not to ever talk to strangers. And if I were to be in real danger and couldn't run away, I was to follow his precise instructions: "Pick up something sharp or heavy in your hands as soon as possible and get ready. Wait for the right moment and strike the enemy. You need to fight back." How can I forget?

I change the channel. "Die Hard 4" is on nine. Where is the Bruce Willis hero when you need one?

My light dinner is in the freezer. "Sometime soon I am going to start cooking again. This is not healthy for me" I say to myself and push the food tray in the microwave.

I take a glimpse at my self-help book on my bedside table. A big fat yawn tumbles out of my mouth, and I know I'm not interested.

I flick through the TV channels to find something less boring while my mind sparks a flashback from lunch time today. This individual was sitting in a corner of the café, pretending to read the papers. I knew better. His eyes were following every breath in the restaurant. Blue eyes marked by steady bushy dark eyebrows. Sexy, I thought. I could not see his torso from where I was sitting but his leather jacket seemed at least one size up. I wondered if it was because of his muscles or else. Still looking good though. But his eyes, hmmm, there was something about his eyes...

I keep pressing the remote control and I hear again "The convict escaped last night from prison, and he is dangerous. Police will reveal his sketch profile in a couple of minutes. Please be aware of potential danger. He may be armed."

This triggers another flashback. One night, three years ago, my partner and I were having a big fight in my old apartment. That was it, I had decided I had enough and showed him the door, but he wouldn't listen to me. Undeterred, I had opened the door in a definitive end of discussion stance, but he got angry and pushed me back. Surprised by his action, I stumbled and fell on the floor, jerking my left knee. "Get out," I shouted eyeballing him, "Now!" He finally left my apartment. The pain brought me back to my senses, I closed the door and started crying. "How could I not see it coming?" I wondered, attending to my knee...

I press the remote control to the next channel.

The microwave beeps and interrupts my reflections. Good, time to eat.

My thoughts go back again to that café earlier today. Something about his deep blue eyes had caught my attention. But why did I have to give him my number so quickly? I don't even remember his name that well. Was it Bob or Rob?? I was busy staring at his lips when he sipped his coffee at my table. Sexy masculine voluptuous lips. And his firm muscles made me think of asking him where he exercised. I'm glad I didn't. Who cares? As long as he liked me and wanted to see me again, that's all that matters. He must have taken an interest; otherwise, why would he go to all that trouble and offer me that beautiful red rose? I turn and smell the rose again; it's sitting on my dining table. Looks beautiful. My thoughts wander for a moment and then I make up my mind.

A quick involuntary look in the mirror and I decide to rush to my purse and search for his number. Why wouldn't I call him first? Why wait? At least I learn he is for real.

So, I dial the number. My heart is pounding. What should I say? Hello, I'm Miranda the young lady you met today at the Soho Café? He might not even remember my name.

Ring, ring. No answer. I try again. No, he is not picking up. I won't leave a message.

Fine. I'll call my best friend Thelma to see how she is going.

Ring. "Hi there, I'm not available at the moment, please leave your name and number at the beep."

Here we go again, nobody is there for me tonight. Fine, I'll pretend I don't care, and I talk to myself pulling faces in the nearby cupboard door mirror.

I flick the remote back on the news and continue to listen. Police released their preliminary sketch description of the fugitive. I take a look at it and my mouth drops down. I look again and start shaking. Those eyes. No, no, no, it can't be. Those eyes look familiar and those bushy eyebrows?! No, this is not happening to me.

I grab my phone and start typing the number on the TV screen. My fingers do not follow my brainwave, wrong number. I try again. My eyes are glued to the TV now, my mind raising, not understanding what it's being said anymore.

That forward-facing man figure on display becomes blurry. How could I be so stupid? I tumble on my bed, my face stares at the ceiling. I must focus. I roll down and drag myself to the bathroom. I manage to bend over the sink and splash some cold water on my face. Feeling a bit better. I start the breathing exercises 1,2,3,4 in, hold, 1,2,3,4 out, and again. I wipe my face and slowly return to my bedroom and pick up my phone. This time I dial correctly and I'm waiting. Line is engaged. Great! Try again. Busy, busy, busy.

What should I do now? The alarm clock shows midnight. Who should I call?

I quickly make up my mind and dial 000. Finally, a female voice answers: "Hello, please state your emergency." I mumble something about the guy I met earlier today at lunch and explain the resemblance with the police sketch on the TV announcement. I am not sure if she understands what I'm saying. She asks for my name and address and tells me to hold on. A police patrol will come in shortly to check things out. Good. I take a deep breath and start rambling my story again, but the phone goes silent. Hello, hello, I keep repeating, not knowing if she hung up on me or put me on hold.

Then it hits me. I remember I gave him my address too, not just my phone number. I'm such an idiot!!! My pupils expand in terror, and my heart starts racing so fast, I'm sure I'll have a coronary.

As I'm standing there, fear-stricken, a slight squeak coming from my door lock draws my attention. I turn and see the door handle moving slightly down from its original position. Oh no! He is coming for me. "Think, don't panic," I encourage myself, in a vain attempt to control my spiralling fearful emotions. Easier said than done. Another squeak sets me into action, and in a panic, I come up with an ad-hoc plan. The kitchen is only two steps away. I snatch the largest and heaviest object in reach, like my father taught me, my biggest heavy-duty Teflon frying pan, and then I quickly and quietly turn off the lights. I hunch down and silently scamper towards the entrance door, holding my breath, endeavouring to regulate my exhaling. I crouch down beside the doorway, silently praying, still hoping I was mistaken, and wait.

The front door handle starts twisting again. I focus for a moment, then rise up and take the stance of a Major League baseball hitter, waiting for a nice fat fast ball down the centre of the plate. I swing forward with all the might I can muster, swivelling and driving with my hips into the strike. HOME RUN! I smash the frying pan into the centre of the door, which reverberates with a dull toning thud. The echo resonates up and down the outside hallway. My arms are sore, and my shoulders are almost dislocated, but I can't afford to scream. I can hardly breathe. I just listen and I'm hearing nothing. I wait with my frying pan held by both my hands, in an attack position, in case he tries again to force himself in.

Nothing. No sounds at all other than the muffled TV from my bedroom.

I wait and wait and wait. Nothing happens. I'm afraid to open the door or check the lobby. So, I slide down on the floor, my back against my entrance door, still clutching at my impromptu weapon with both hands. Ten, fifteen minutes pass. I'm still waiting in silence.

At this point, the adrenaline is gone. I doze on and off for what appears to have been only a few seconds.

Something wakes me up. I hear footsteps echoing in the stairwell, sprinted footsteps as if someone is in a hurry. I freak out. I grab my frying pan again, straighten my body, and stand by for attack, holding my breath for the second shot.

Incessant knocks pepper my door. "Open up please, Police!" A voice breaks out through the rampant pounding on the door.

I freeze. My ears can't process the call until the third worrying appeal ends. I nervously check the peephole of my door and then slowly and cautiously open it.

Standing in front of me in the lobby are two of Sydney's finest police officers with concerned looks, staring at me. "Ms Jones? "The tall one asks. "Yes" I reply slowly exhaling the breath I had been holding in for a short while, downing the frypan to my right hip level at the same time, and resting my left hand up on the door frame.

"Are you alright?" they ask me, and they introduce themselves.

"Yes, I'm OK, thanks," I reply in a trance.

I look down and see someone's figure laying on the floor, between the two officers. The second officer, holding a flashlight pointed towards the individual lounged in front of my door, appears to be checking for a pulse. My eyes nearly jump out of their sockets when suddenly I understand the gravity of the situation, I'm finding myself in. I gasp for air, which instantly explodes from my lungs with a wheezing sound. I start hyperventilating.

The first officer, the tall one, attempts to come to my aid as I continually fail to catch my breath.

"Please try to breathe in and out slowly," he says. "In and out, slowly," he repeats, holding my arms and mimicking the procedure. I'm following his instructions, looking into his eyes, and slowly I recover.

"I'm sorry to ask you this!" he continues. As he steadies me in an upright position, leaning towards the wall, and unhurriedly taking the frying pan off my hand, he asks "Do you know this person?"

I look down to inspect the intruder lying down in the dark lobby, near my doorstep. The second officer kneels by him and dials the number for the Ambulance Services. Then he turns his torch onto the stranger's face, to help me see him better. My mind is racing, the whole episode of this evening's events has seriously caused a slow-motion effect to my brain.

"No, I don't think so." Then something about the man's eyebrows registers with me and a sudden burst of adrenaline sets me into gear back again.

"Oh, my God, that's Bob." I blurt out, involuntarily covering my mouth with my right palm. "I met him earlier today at lunch in the city. He seemed nice," my words spill out. "Is he alright?" I ask. The second officer shrugs his shoulders.

"He seems unconscious. What happened?" he enquires. "Did you hit him?"

"NNNooo", I stammer. "I thought I heard someone attempting to break in, and I smashed the door with my frying pan from inside. I didn't know what else to do". The first officer looks at me like I had two heads, while the other one turns his head away. I thought I heard a giggle.

The tall one recollects his professional persona and gently places his hand on my shoulder and says, "We are really sorry this happened to you, but you'll have to come with us to the station for a statement."

"OK, sure," I mumble, still clearly in shock.

The second officer is now leaning towards the unwelcomed visitor, checking his pulse again, and examining him carefully. "It looks like he fainted," he adds.

Then he turns to me and says: "You're lucky." He pauses. "He escaped from prison this morning. His ex-partner reported him to the Police for having attacked her this afternoon that resulted in an injury for her. Did you hear anything by any chance? She lives right there on the other side of the hallway, on the same floor as you."

"No, I was at work all day, I wasn't home," I reply in a blur.

He continues "He was probably hiding out here, waiting for her return or maybe he was just looking for a new target. We don't know yet. We traced his phone to this address. And when we received your 000 call, we rushed here as quickly as we could. Though it looks like it we weren't quick enough."

Tears are rolling down my face as my eyes turn slowly towards the beautiful red rose sitting on my dining table, finally feeling relieved.

Ring of Hook

A gripping tale about one of Ireland's oldest landmarks.

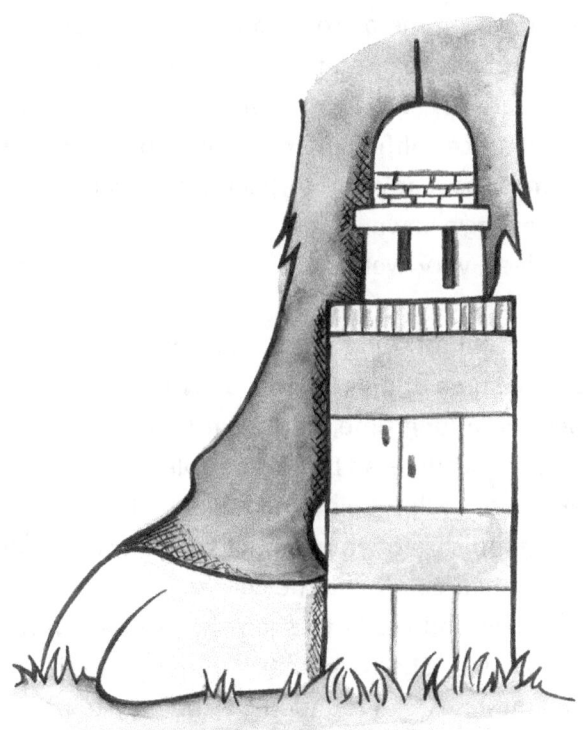

On a sunny Sunday morning, I found myself calling my good friend and neighbour, Joan, to invite her for a walk on the beach, our favourite stroll. Joan is a tall elderly lady, blonde, with beautiful piercing blue eyes, going on 81 years old soon, not that you would guess by checking out her slender figure and great sense of humour.

She was sporting a light blue quilted vest, matching her eyes, over a long white sleeve top, and a pair of jeans, looking sharp.

We met at the street corner as per usual.

"You're a great storyteller, Joan." I complimented her.

"It's probably something to do with my Irish roots" she giggled.

There was always a tale ready to unfold about her family or people she knew back home in Ireland. You would think a leprechaun tale was woven into almost every Irish fellow's existence.

She started telling me a story about an enigmatic lighthouse she knew of, that nobody wanted to go to anymore due to its unsettling mysteries. Apparently, the lighthouse keepers had disappeared one day without a trace, although the light continued to shine in the night. Hmmm... too early for this kind of weary gloom for me, I thought, repressing a yawn.

Couldn't sleep very well the night before, too much binging on Netflix.

"Oh, I almost forgot", she said smiling at me. "I'm going to spend some time with some of my relatives up North in Queensland, whom I haven't seen in a long time, and from there I'm going on a cruise around the East Coastline, so I won't be able to see you for a while".

"How exciting," I said. "Enjoy and take care!"

"You take good care of yourself; I'll see you when I get back" she added and disappeared around the corner.

Always smiling and ready to share her stories with anyone who would care to listen. She had a gift, I thought. I felt good after our weekly encounters. Me, grounded in the day-to-day life realities, Joan, unravelling great life experiences and learnings. Good balance, I chuckled.

Once home, I went about my daily Sunday routine of doing absolutely nothing. Marvelous.

A glass of Chardy in my hand, lounging comfortably in my armchair in my cosy Sydney home, on a lazy day like that, it was perfect. I was enjoying the moment.

Spring was on its way, that fresh new feeling when everything seems possible, especially after a long lingering coldish winter.

As I was browsing the web - daily habit - my fingers typed in "lighthouse" on a whim. Various images popped up. The Ring of Hook lighthouse was one of them. One of the oldest lighthouses in the world. Hmmm. It must have been 30 years since my last journey to Ireland.

Then, suddenly I remembered I had some hand notes, stashed in a folder somewhere.

"Going through some old stuff could be fun" I convinced myself and started looking for the papers.

At the back of the last drawer, in the last possible place to look for it, there it was. A handwritten journal about my trip to the Ring of Hook, 30 years ago. As I placed the file on my lap, a picture fell off and landed at my feet. Ring of Hook again. Coincidence?

I started reading the notes, and it all came back to me like it was yesterday...How could I ever forget?

It was my third time in Ireland, back in 1999, when my friend Sarah invited me to visit her parents in Arklow. On a sunny Saturday morning, Sarah and I casually dressed jumped in her car, sunglasses on, and negotiated our way out of Dublin....Such a vivid memory now.

No hint of rain, no veil of clouds. "Incredible," I mused.

By the time we reached her parents' home we were starving. Soup and roast lamb, flanked by green peas, carrots, and hearty potatoes, followed by my favourite dessert: jelly, ice cream and bananas.

I could see it all, like in a movie reeling in front of me.

Sarah extended an enticing invitation: a journey to the magic Hook Head lighthouse, known as the Ring of Hook, one of the oldest lighthouses in the world. We like that idea, so we all decided to go.

Our imagination was running wild. So many stories were going around about that place...

The sky's clarity shifted, and soon raindrops started dancing in the air. Ireland's weather, as always, fully unpredictable.

We passed by Wexford, a town bustling with life and energy. Quick break to stretch our legs, and we continued our journey. The sky's deep blue tones transitioned to blue-grey shades, the green fields flanking the road, equally spectacular.

En route, we passed by cattle leisurely grazing beside an ancient, timeworn stone church. Tranquillity at its best, like a frozen moment in time.

As we approached Rosslare Harbour, we knew we had taken the wrong turn. Sarah's mother urged us not to give up; we listened.

By the time we dwindled into a narrow, rustic byway, it was getting late. Tiny cottages popped up, filled with weeds pushing through the cracks. Irish leprechaun folklore whooshed through my mind. I can still remember that feeling.

The air became chilly as the sun was setting further.

Then this big three-story mansion emerged on the horizon. My gaze locked onto it. Sarah's father, following my line of sight, began to unfold a tale that had shrouded a mansion called Loftus Hall in a cloak of mystery for generations:

"Long ago Loftus Hall belonged to a wealthy landlord, known for his lavish parties and late-night card games. As tales of those opulent gatherings spread, guests were lured to his manor, curious to learn more about the feasts and luxury.

One fateful night, an enigmatic figure walked in the door and attended the games, winning one after another. The landlord grew suspicious and moved closer to this visitor to scrutinise him. At that point, his eldest daughter who was also attending the card game that night accidentally dropped a card. When she bent down to pick it up, she looked beneath the table and saw that the mysterious man had a cloven foot, a symbol of evil. It was then that she stood up and cried out loud: "You have a cloven foot!" Breathless gasps swelled through the room as the outsider vanished into the night through the roof, leaving behind a large hole in the ceiling.

From then onwards, misfortune unfolded. Livestock perished, crops faded, and the once-prosperous manor house started to decline. Some spoke of the landlord's wife's untimely death and his eldest daughter losing her mind, a tragedy. People stopped going to the Loftus Hall and the landlord eventually ran into debt. The once-vibrant house surrendered to eerie silence.

A sense of anxiety persisted, an unspoken belief that the mansion was haunted. Over time, two different orders of nuns were set up, but they didn't last long.

Then, in the 1980s, a brief local initiative emerged in the form of a pub. Yet even the pub attempt was unable to bring the big house back to life. And so, the mansion endured in isolation."

As the clock ticked 7.30 pm, our journey along the cliffs continued. The waves, relentlessly crashed against the rocky road's edges, winding lace that clung to the coastline. Neither the water nor the land would yield—an ongoing battle competing for supremacy. Picture perfect.

Then the silhouette of the mysterious Hook lighthouse surfaced on the horizon, a sentinel of the sea. This old-age structure, adorned in stern black and white, stood as a steadfast guardian of ships in the waters of the Ocean Celtic Sea for over 800 years.

We arrived at the car park almost in darkness. Undaunted, we climbed the slippery rocks towards the lighthouse, facing the relentless wind with determination. Up top, we paused for a few moments. The roar of the waves and the howling wind left my ears soaring. Unforgettable sensation to this day.

That was when Sarah's mom began to tell us the story of the Ring of Hook:

"Many years ago, there was a solitary man who lived in this remote place. The lighthouse keeper was a man of few words, who dedicated his life to lighting the towering beacon every evening at precisely the same time. The nearby villagers thought he was a bit strange, an eccentric recluse, but they left him alone, as he never bothered them with anything.

Yet whispers of strange encounters wandered throughout the village at times. Hushed conversations spoke of unexplained voices echoing from the direction of the lighthouse during some nights. A few brave men approached the lighthouse keeper with their inquiries, only to be met with denials. Over time, their incursions faded into the background noise of their everyday life, until the lighthouse keeper was no longer seen around.

Gradually, he became a distant memory and the village forgot about him entirely.

One fateful day, a passerby who had taken a tour around the tower, descended to the treacherous cliffside, and inadvertently broke his left leg. His distressing screams reverberated through the rugged terrain, but no one came to his aid. As he slowly succumbed to his pain, he drifted into unconsciousness. When he awoke, the pitch-black night surrounded him. No one in sight.

At 8.00pm sharp, a beam of light pierced the darkness from the lighthouse. Was it real or was he hallucinating?

Mustering all his strength, he clawed his way through the rocks and shrubs in searing pain, until he reached the lighthouse entrance door. It wasn't locked. He pulled himself inside, and cried out for help again, to no reply. He teetered on the brink of consciousness. In the depths of the night, he thought he heard some faint voices. Was he delirious? He wasn't sure.

At dawn, he gathered his last dwindling energy, pushed himself outside and leaned against the lighthouse's cold stone wall, still hoping that someone would come. Hours passed. Just as he had lost all his hope, a random early morning tourist passed by and heard his faint cries and rushed him to the hospital. News of his ordeal spread throughout the village like wildfire, reigniting long-buried rumours.

A group of young locals, determined to unravel the mystery of the lighthouse once and for all, embarked on a late daylight expedition. They observed the lighthouse walls and waited in anticipation for the clock to strike eight. There it was: the light was on. And yet no lighthouse keeper emerged, no voices were heard, no answers were found. They departed, swearing never to return. And since, every night, the tower's light continued to shine."

As we made our way back to the parking lot, deep in thought, Sarah's father complained about the chilly breeze and urged us to leave.

Once in the car, I stole a final glimpse at the lighthouse. That day had raised more questions than answers for me...I promised I would try to find out more.

And here I am, back in Sydney, 30 years later, sitting in my lounge still pondering with the idea of finding out more about the Ring of Hook.

Where to start?

Browsing the net, I found some tales of past keepers who had vanished without a trace. Not much to go on. Days turned into weeks, weeks into months. One day, a breakthrough: while seeping through the NSW State Library archives, I stumbled over a long-lost journal, written by a former lighthouse keeper of the Hook, named Peter McGregor. He thoroughly recorded his years of tending to the lighthouse and mentioned some strange voices that had haunted the tower. Nothing new.

Not knowing where else to turn to, I decided to start a website blog, asking people for their help. You never know, I mused. I invited anyone who could provide any information about the Ring of Hook history to contact me directly. Long shot, but why not?

To my surprise two weeks later I received an email from this guy, Ben, with an attachment—a photograph of Ring of Hook. His message read: "The light still shines, and the secrets endure. Here is my number. Please call me. Regards, Ben". Who was this mysterious messenger from Dublin?

Filled with excitement, I called Ben the next day, not knowing what to expect.

It turns out Ben was the great-grandson of Peter McGregor, a former keeper of the Ring of Hook lighthouse. Wait, what?! I heard that name before in the library archives. I felt like I'd hit the jackpot, after so many years.

Ben was an elderly soft-spoken man, whose 14-year-old niece had found my web blog on the internet and asked him to contact me. Luckily, he did. Realising this was not a hoax, I asked him if we could discuss our views about the subject prior to making any further commitments. He agreed. I went through the archives I've discovered at the NSW State Library with him and shared my own encounter with the Ring of Hook many years ago. He was delighted. The more we spoke the more we realised we had so much in common. Ben was equally enthusiastic to disclose his own family trails and insights connected to the lighthouse with me as I was genuinely interested in learning more about Ring of Hook's history and connection to his own ancestors. I was thrilled.

Finally, I will be able to shed some light on this old pursuit that nagged me for over 30 years, and I was not alone in this quest. Better late than never.

We arranged to meet up at the lighthouse's entrance, two weeks after our last online chat.

Time flew by quickly when I started my preparations for the trip. Very exciting. Reasonable accommodation. Flights booked, a short stopover in London. Not looking forward to the 26-hour flight, but you can't have everything.

On arrival at Dublin Airport, I picked up my car rental from the Hertz desk, then packed myself off to my hotel to shake off the jetlag. Two days later, I found myself retracing my ride from Dublin to the Ring of Hook from 30 years ago. How exhilarating.

And there it was, the tower standing tall as ever. Its reflection in the clear water pool surrounding the adjacent cliffs a beautiful extension of its majestic beauty. It hasn't changed at all. It was like I never left. Memories spun through my mind vividly. So many other things have changed since last time I was there. Sarah's parents had since passed away and Sarah and I stayed in contact occasionally. I never returned to Ireland after that trip, and yet the stories they told me on that special day on our way to the Hook had lodged deeply in my conscience and ultimately ignited my quest for finding out more about that amazing place.

Ben arrived on time, at midday, as agreed, carrying a weathered bundle of letters and some additional journals that had been passed down to him through his family. We set down on a sheltered cleft, overlooking the sea, and went through them one by one. The documents unveiled a similar story: Peter had heard mysterious voices during his tenure but chose to keep them secret, fearing people's judgement.

Ben and I went on an exploration tour around the tower, retracing Peter's footsteps from his writings. Our imagination ran freely for a few minutes. Then, we looked at each other and wondered: "What now? Should we unveil Peter's notes? Would people still fear the Ring of Hook's lingering scary stories?" Understandably Ben wanted to protect his great–grandfather's name and reputation.

We discussed the pros and cons for a couple of hours and, eventually, we decided to approach the local authorities the next day and test the waters. Remarkably we were in luck. Despite our doubts, the authorities paid attention to us. They informed us that they had undertaken independent research and uncovered a link to another family. This family was connected to a man named Liam O'Brien, whose children had chosen to follow in their father's footsteps and become lightkeepers as well.

Although the lighthouse was now automated, and there were no lightkeepers anymore, the family connection with the lighthouse landscape continued. The Council officers organised a meeting with the local community to gauge their reaction on making all these findings public.

We waited feverishly for another week for the outcome. The villagers agreed, it was time to make the letters public and embrace the Ring of Hook's heritage. They understood their unique value.

Once the decision was made, things moved on quickly. They set up a crowd-funded project on the website to restore the lighthouse to its former glory. Also, a small room near the entrance was built up and turned into a makeshift museum, with some additional amenities for tourists, where they displayed the Ring of Hook's archives for visitors and history fans to enjoy. Only guided tours were permitted inside. They dedicated it to Peter McGregor and all the families who had ties to the lighthouse over centuries, to honour their lives and to acknowledge their efforts for documenting the history of the place. A Ring of Hook website ensued.

The best legacy possible for Ben's great-grandfather came true. Ben was radiant with joy.

Unsurprisingly the lighthouse became a popular tourist destination over time. Once a source of fear and apprehension, Ring of Hook was now standing as a symbol of collective legacy and pride.

"Great outcome" I thought, on my flight back to Sydney.

Joan, my good friend, had returned from her cruise around the East Coast by now. I couldn't wait to tell her about my latest adventure. I called her and anxiously arranged a time for our walk the same day.

There she was, happy and chatty as always. The cruise must have been full of great events by the sound of it. Finally, I found an opening and started telling her about my recent trip to Ireland.

She paused. The moment I mentioned my Ring of Hook quest, her eyes sparkled with curiosity. I was so excited about my recent adventure. I told her about how I met Ben, how we went there together, how we met with the local authorities and how we obtained recognition for that historic place. She listened quietly, and suddenly, her eyes filled with tears.

"What's wrong?" I asked in disdain. "Have I said something wrong?"

"No, not at all", she replied. "When I was a kid, my grandma used to take me to the Ring of Hook. She told me so many stories about that spot. I was always listening to her in awe. I think I shared some of them with you before. In those days, no one dared to visit the lighthouse as they all believed it was haunted. Not my grandma".

"Enjoy its beauty while it lasts" she used to say to me, "and forget about what other people think."

Joan caught her breath for a moment and continued "I always thought that place deserved much more than those unrelenting whispers of fear. I am so glad you and Ben brought its legacy back to light, for everyone to see and appreciate its true value and heritage. Thank you so much," and she gave me a hug.

The Things You Get Used to

A group of students embark on a tour that unexpectedly takes them to Dracula's Castle where they experience a series of unusual events.

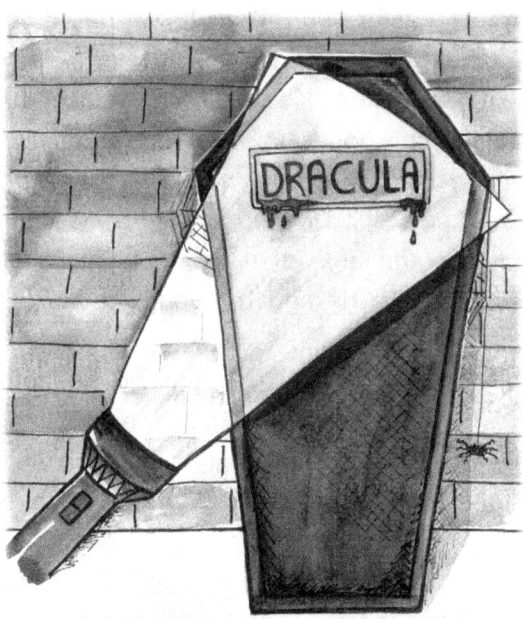

Here is a story about my first tour with my choir group in the winter of 1981, a time when frosty winds seemed to conspire against us. An unforgettable journey was about to unfold.

We left by bus from our University Cultural Centre in Bucharest on a bitterly chilly winter morning, sometime around Christmas, to a place called Bran village, close to Dracula Castle, in Transylvania, present-day Romania.

For those of you who haven't heard of the Dracula legend before, here is its summary in a nutshell: "Dracula" is a classic horror novel written by Irish author Bram Stoker, first published in 1897. Some argue that Bran Castle was Stoker's inspiration for Dracula's home in his book. The novel's enduring popularity has led to countless adaptations in various media. Stoker's horror novel inflamed imaginations, and decades later, on the silver screen, the word Dracula became synonymous with vampire. A popular theory among critics is that the character Count Dracula was based on the infamous ruler Vlad III, better known as Vlad the Impaler, governor of Walachia. Historic records talk about Vlad impaling his enemies on stakes to consolidate his political power and for defending his people from foreign invasion. Unconfirmed accounts claim that he sometimes drank their blood. Whether Vlad truly drank blood or not no one knows, but the legend has it that the infamous vampire Dracula lived in Bran Castle and the vampire stories persisted for centuries.

Our choir tour was supposed to last for two days, but we didn't hit the road until we crammed in everything we could carry. The stage costumes didn't fit in the luggage compartment, so we lined them up on hangers in the back row, and playfully called them the "wardrobe".

It was warm and cozy inside the bus, people were in high spirits, cracking jokes, defying the snow, and freezing cold outside. I lounged comfortably in my seat and mentally prepared for the journey.

Two hours later it was already getting dark. Snow was falling like something out of a fairy tale. The bus sped through the towns and villages on our route without stopping. We needed to reach our destination by 5pm for our musical performance.

Then the weather suddenly took a turn for the worse. Large snowflakes were crashing on the foggy windshield, swirling in shiny twists under the spotlight's glow. Roaring wind added its dramatic tunes to the winter's gig around us. All that was missing were the howling wolves to complete the scene.

We pressed on towards Bran village through the dark afternoon. Vampire thoughts crossed my mind, but I swiftly brushed them aside. Gradually my initial optimism dampened, and an uneasiness settled in. I glanced through the icy windows at the ominous night. No one else was on the road but us. In time, the heat inside the bus started to fade, so we bundled together to keep warm. Conversations dwindled until they stopped completely.

The bus struggled to climb the hill road as it faced increasingly abundant snowdrifts. The driver carefully maneuvered the vehicle, but ice glistened on the road, and it started sliding. Then the engine sputtered and eventually the heating system broke down. "Great! What else could go wrong?" I thought.

The chill became so intense that we trembled like birds that had ignored to migrate to warmer climates, and soon enough, we were chattering our teeth. Some enthusiasts brought out their bottles of alcohol to warm up. George, the choir conductor, would normally not allow us to indulge in any type of alcohol, but on this occasion, he made an exception.

Gradually, the good mood of the bus's inhabitants returned. We took bets on our potential arrival time, a Johnnie Walker bottle as the grand prix. As tiredness kicked in, some passengers nodded off, leaning forward on their palms; we nicknamed them the "clock repairmen" and the others, resting face up on their seat backrests, the "star readers."

Slowly, we started preparing ourselves for the upcoming performance and practiced some vocal exercises.

All of a sudden, we hear a hissssss... a tire burst. "Here we go, flat tire" cried the driver erupting in an unflattering charade.

The bus came to a halt. All our recovered enthusiasm vanished immediately when he tried to open the front door. He couldn't even step outside on the first attempt due to the wind gust. A few choir members jammed together behind him and when the door cracked open again, they shoved the cranky driver into the snowy dunes. Diana, our lead singer, followed him out in the snow. Then, one by one, four other guys jumped off in the dark to help change the tire. The rest of us huddled together to keep warm.

At some point we heard a sharp scream: "Ouch!" It was Diana, signalling us that she had twisted her left knee and needed help to get back in. Aiding hands pulled her out from the snow. She was massaging her knee vigorously, clearly in pain, but when asked, she confirmed with a gesture she'd be alright.

With a new tire in place, we continued our journey. It didn't take long until nature called, and we needed to take a pee stop. An awkward situation. Snow heaps piled alongside the road, made the climb towards some privacy hunt difficult, plus nobody entertained the idea of going into the woods. Boys and girls looked at each other until George's powerful voice cried out loudly from behind: "Boys on the left side of the bus, girls on the right. Please hurry up!" We took a plunge and followed his instructions.

From time to time, I could hear Diana's anguish in the back of the bus. Someone recommended she'd take some painkillers, and she did.

"What else might go wrong today?" I found myself wondering again.

After less than half an hour of strenuous climbing, the bus thermostat jammed. The engine was overheating and could have given out at any moment if we didn't let it cool down." Here we go again" the driver sobbed in despair.

So, we stopped for fifteen minutes, drove for another fifteen, on and off and on again to help the engine cool off. A well-fed snail could have overtaken us if they dared adventure outside that night.

Some of us started singing a popular song called "In the forest, dear forest," fitting in the context, passing time.

At one juncture, we all thought we had lost our way, but the driver was adamant we were fine. Someone flicked a lighter and checked his watch, and we realized how late it was. We lost hope that anyone would still be waiting for us to perform that night.

At that point, Diana, our lead singer, burst into tears unexpectedly and cried: "I can't deal with this pain anymore. I need a doctor."

"Great! What do we do now?" I worried.

Luckily enough the driver remembered a shortcut to Dracula Castle, and decided to take the turn from the main road so we could ask for help. Five minutes later, we were in luck. There it was! The castle was standing tall in front of us in the misty night. Its stone walls and turrets projected an impressive silhouette against the backdrop of the Carpathian Mountains. Massive and dimly lit, it appeared gloomy but sublime.

The bus came to a halt. George, the conductor, rushed up the rocky path and banged with all his might at Dracula's Castle front gate. Some of us followed him in silence.

Minutes stretched into an agonising wait, and just when our hope waned, the heavy wooden door creaked open.

This slim silhouette cloaked in shadows asked us in a voice that seemed like an echo from the past:

"Hello, travellers. How can I assist you on this fateful night?" An eerie chill swept down my spine.

George explained Diana's condition, and the mysterious figure let us in, then turned around and hurried to give the village doctor a call.

We stepped into this cold dark courtyard and then followed the castle caretaker's steps through a tiny but thick wooden door into a hallway. It felt like we were stepping back in time. Once inside he switched on the lights and I gasped for air once I noticed a big black coffin, on my left-hand side, lined up to the wall, bearing Dracula's name on it. I froze, so did the others.

The castle guardian returned quickly. He followed our gaze and said: "My dear travellers, fear not, that coffin is just a prop for visitors" he chuckled.

Two colleagues brought Diana into the hallway on their arms and set her down on an archaic oak chest covered in a black mantle bearing the castle crest. She was in agony, poor thing. We felt for her. They strapped up her knee as best they could with some makeshift T-shirt bandages to alleviate the pain and asked her to stay still. We were waiting in silence for the doctor to arrive acquainting ourselves with the surroundings.

The caretaker, now our improvised tour guide, started to tell us about the castle, with its 57 rooms and numerous secret corridors usually not open to the public. On the spur of the moment, I asked if it would be possible to show us one of those mysterious hidden passageways while we were waiting for the doctor, and to my surprise he agreed. I followed him to this tiny crevasse in a side wall, barely noticeable for an untrained eye in that low-lit spot, and before I knew it, I stepped into this chilly entranceway leading to one of the watchtowers. Five of us took the challenge. The wizened old caretaker handed out some sturdy, but functional flashlights. A quick equipment checks to ensure the flashlights were working, and we were ready. Then he turned to us with a beckoning wave of his arm, to follow him. "This way folks and watch your step"!

We had not walked more than what it felt like twenty steps, when a huge deafening bang filled the corridor. We all jumped and screamed with fear.

"What was that?" stammered Fiona, in panic-induced shock.

The old caretaker looked back over his shoulder with a slight grin.

"Fear not, my dear travellers! I sometimes leave some windows open in the rooms that run adjacent to this passageway. That's just the wind blowing a door closed, you get used to it after a while".

As we were climbing up the steep twisted steps one behind the other, a thick spider web clutched at my clothes out of nowhere and almost touched my face. I gasped instantly. Then a shiver ran down my spine, I wouldn't dare complain. My gloves came in handy to wipe the web off. "I can't take much more of this" I promised myself.

On the final approach to the doorway of the watchtower, our legs were aching from the arduous hike. Unexpectedly the girl in the lead, Andrea, stumbled on one of the steps and dropped the flashlight she was holding. A flying creature darted out of a crack in the wall over the heads.

"Ah" screamed Andrea. "It's a vampire bat! "

The wizened old caretaker shone the light on his face and looked sternly at Andrea. "Fear not, my dear traveller, you'll find that's just a little bird, who nests up here in the winter months. I've been the caretaker here for over 40 years, and I've never seen a vampire bat". He shrugged. "Guests sometimes see strange things. I just listen to them. You get used to it after a while!"

We all exchanged glances as if to say, "That was a big wingspan for a little bird."

Andrea picked up the flashlight, which luckily was still working, turned towards me, and said, "Something brushed against my head, that's why I fell and dropped the torch, it scared the hell out of me." I shone my flashlight around the area we just traversed and noticed several garlands of garlic shrouding the entrance to the watchtower.

"Hmmm, what's with all the garlic?" I asked in surprise.

The wily old caretaker replied with his standard opening line. "Fear not, my dear traveller, the garlic is to ward off the vampires."

"Wait, what"? Came the reply from both Andrea and me simultaneously. "I thought vampires don't exist" I startled.

"Well, that's what we tell the tourists!" He chuckled as he continued to lead us on to the battlements of the watchtower. "You get used to it after a while!"

Once at the top it became clear that the castle was built on these rocky precipices, commanding spectacular views, although I couldn't see much in the dark. Imagination ran wild for a few minutes. A flying creature flew past our eyelines, its figure reflecting against the moonlight which had started to find a gap in the cloud cover.

"That's a big bloody bird," I mumbled. "It really did not look like a bat."

Before long, the gap in the clouds began to seal shut once more, the moonlight fading as rapidly as it had initially emerged. I took that as a sign to head back.

Almost like reading my mind, the old caretaker announced, "Probably time we move back to your companions".

In the doorway to the corridor back down, I had a final glance out on the battlements, and in my peripheral vision, I caught a glimpse of the "little bird;" the backdrop of the dying moonlight, gave me a clearer inspection. "That's way too big to be a bird!" my thoughts racing. But as I've never seen a vampire bat before, I put it down to just a flying creature.

I followed my mates down the steps, my flashlight's beam bouncing off the stone walls of the winding narrow old corridors.

"Are we going the right way?" wondered Michael, checking around.

"Fear not, my dear travellers" came the standard reply.

"I really wished he'd come up with a new saying by that time," I thought "this one was getting on my nerves."

"Just taking another secret passageway; this one will bring us outside the castle, near the front gates!" came his enthusiastic reply. "I haven't had the chance to come back this way with guests for some time! I don't get a chance to show anyone these little treasures, but…"

"You get used to it after a while" came the reply of five of us in unison.

As we all stepped out of the doorway, held open politely by the caretaker, we all heard him say warningly: "Watch your step, the ground can be slippery here".

The unmistakable clatter of horse hooves resounded on the snowy road. "What the hell is that?" exclaimed Andrea as she pointed out into the night. A faint glimmer of light poked through the darkness and started to gleam brighter and brighter, just as the sound of horses' hooves grew louder, now accompanied by the jingling of a bell.

When the light and sounds reached their crescendo, we were able to make out the clear image of a sleigh being drawn by two roan draft horses. An old-style kerosene lantern lighting up the horses' shiny coats, as they snorted and strained against the harnesses.

The sleigh came to a sliding stop next to us, and a middle-aged man, rugged up in a winter sheepskin long coat leaned over and asked, "Anyone looking for a doctor?" His fur cap with ear flaps fastened under his chin caught my eye. "This is one strange place!" I thought as I observed the doctor picking up his medical bag and entering the courtyard at a frenetic pace.

Diana had slipped in a nap. The painkillers helped. The doctor opened his bag and gently woke her up. She was still in pain, so he started checking her vitals. When he touched her injured knee, she sobbed, an involuntary knee-jerk reaction. He carefully examined it and advised: "It's a knee strain. I'll put on some knee braces for now and give you an injection for the pain" he added." But you will have to see a specialist when you get back home."

By the time the doctor finished packing up his stuff, we had stashed away our torches and started to prepare for departure. Diana was already feeling much better and heaved a sigh of relief. I felt happy for her. Things could have turned out much worse. She was able to stand up and hop along as we were ready to leave.

We thanked the doctor profusely, for his unique ambulance service. He acknowledged us graciously, turned around and left the room, his ear flaps untied.

At that point, we were heading to the exit door ourselves when suddenly, everything went completely pitch black. Lights off!

"Creepy! Was this Dracula's spirit not wanting to let his uninvited guests leave his place so quickly?" I shivered.

The caretaker blurred in the dark: "Fear not, my dear travellers. It's just a power surge, it happens all the time, especially on a stormy night like this. I have a candle somewhere close, wait here."

"Are you serious, where would we go? ", thoughts swirling through my head.

A match flickered and he returned quickly with a trembling candlelight, but the wait felt like centuries passed. "He looks like the hermit in the tarot cards," I imagined.

"It happens," he repeated when he returned, "but you get used to it after a while!"

We thanked our somewhat strange but kind host for his services, he simply nodded in acknowledgment in the candlelight glint. As we left the castle shrouded in utter darkness, we couldn't help but wonder if we had encountered a spirit of the past who had come to our aid in a time of need, or we were just lucky.

Finally, we went back on the road to the show, when not long after we left, someone spotted a lantern, and some random houses scattered around, almost snowed under. That was Bran village! We couldn't believe it! We arrived at our destination *only* 4 hours late!! The bus stopped in the middle of the road, puffing in the heavy snow. We slowly strode down the empty street toward the Community Cultural Centre guided by its stubborn street light pole at the entrance.

Not a soul in sight. Inside the centre, a drowsy guard was preparing to lock up the place. When he spotted us, he wasn't pleased. George explained what happened and asked what to do. The grumpy building's administrator called the show producer for advice and left us there to our own devices.

Tired, cold, and hungry, we waited in silence.

Only five minutes later, the "decision-maker" appeared with a big smile on his face. He apologised for not waiting for us, rubbed his hands together as in "we are in business," and asked George:

"How long do you need to get ready?"

"Are you kidding me? It is already 9.00pm." I wondered.

"Where is the audience?" George replied.

"Don't you worry about that," the organiser said. "Ready in half an hour?"

"OK," George confirmed. He turned towards us and added: "You have 20 minutes to gear up for the show. Ladies and gentlemen, to the dressing rooms, please"

"What dressing rooms? There were none." I muttered.

We fidgeted for about 15 minutes; costumes, and makeup on, all in one room, and we were ready to go.

Through a frosted side window, I noticed dark silhouettes ambling back to the concert hall through the heavy snow. In no time the hall was packed. "I would very much like to have that kind of public reaction when I'll launch my first book!" I joked to myself.

As the curtain ascended, a frenzy of applause erupted. "Greetings! Greetings!"

We started playing our beloved repertoire. The audience immediately caught up with the rhythm and the melody and kept clapping. We succeeded in thrilling the late-night spectators to the point where they joined in singing along with us. Happy faces everywhere.

While I was playing my part, a man in the audience wearing a fur cap with ear flaps up caught my attention. To my surprise it was the doctor whom we had met just minutes earlier! "How intriguing! Going from saving lives to being a music lover" I chuckled.

The final song turned into joyful chaos. Thunderous applause followed by repeated cheers. Everyone was having a great time.

We bowed with joy, thanking the wonderful spectators several times as we bid farewell. We were tired but so were they.

And then, the inevitable happened: the lights went off in the concert hall. "No, not again!" I whined in a muffled voice.

People were sitting patiently in their chairs, waiting in the dark. After a few moments, a feeling of unease started to creep in, just as this familiar voice of the castle taker resonated from the rear, "Fear not, folks. It's just a power surge, it happens all the time, you will get used to it after a while!"

"Urgh!" I exclaimed.

It didn't take long though, and the lights came back on. Everybody cheered, "Hooray!"

My colleagues and I looked at each other for a short while, shrugged our shoulders as in "it is what it is" and prepared to get off the stage, while people in the audience were still sporadically clapping at us as we exited.

I attempted to spot the castle caretaker at the back so I could bid farewell with a wave, but he eluded my sight. "Hmmm" I wondered "Where did he go?"

After the curtain fell and the applause faded, I felt like this unique trip was more than just a tour. It had become a winter night's journey into the unfamiliar, where fantasy and reality had intertwined.

As I made my way out, I couldn't resist stealing a moment to peak through a side window of the concert hall and take in the beauty of this wilderness landscape. It had stopped snowing by then and the moon had started to shine its light again through a break in the clouds, just like it did on the battlements.

Dracula's Castle etched against the night sky was clearly visible in the moonlight, including the watchtower I had visited only a few hours ago.

Something darted across the sky. "Was it a bird or a bat?" I wondered. The answer puzzled me as the cryptic words of the wizened elderly caretaker reverberated in my ears "You get used to it after a while!"

A Special Journey to Uluru

An extraordinary visit to Uluru, where human connections could transcend time.

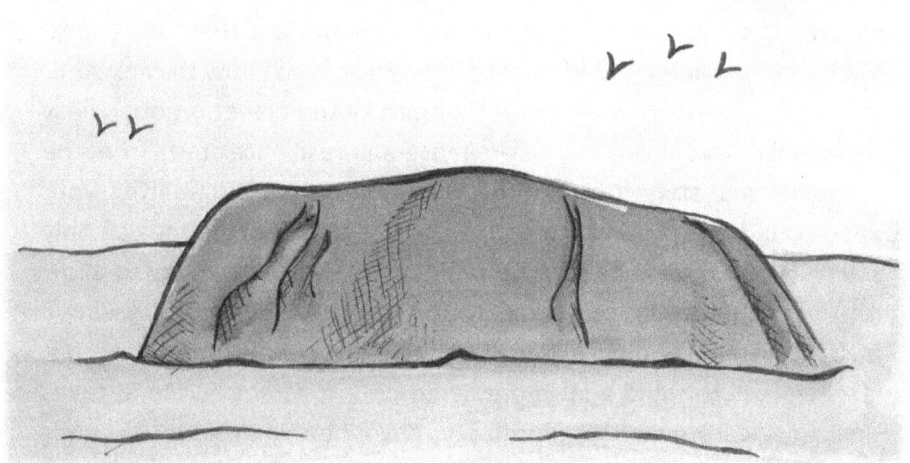

As an immigrant I found adapting to the Aussie way of life challenging at times. So many things to learn, so many changes to deal with, so many challenges to overcome. For a while, I felt like I was suspended in a transitioning world all by myself. I went through various stages of transformation, from denial, shock, resistance to acceptance and new beginning. It can be a hard experience but so rewarding at the same time. I'm not talking about travelling as a tourist for a limited time to a different country, knowing that at some point you'll go back home where you are safe, wherever back home is for you. I'm talking about that step in your life when turning back is no longer an option, whether the decision to go somewhere else was made for you by chance, or you made it yourself due to certain circumstances. Whichever the case may be, it requires lots of courage and determination to take that leap into the unknown.

The beauty of it all is that, at the end of the day, it is a great experience, and that no matter the hardships and barriers you may face, it provides you with a new perspective of the world. And that is worth exploring. There are so many new things out there waiting to be discovered and learned, that you may not even know they existed.

Coming to Australia from another part of the planet is not an easy experience. The journey of self-reliance and resilience starts from the moment you step foot on this vast continent. No matter your background, age, or any other previous life experiences, one can only start "living" in their new world reality when they are ready to allow it to happen. Finding your way around Sydney, for example, taking a bus or a train, finding a job, meeting new people, mastering the language, all this and a lot more could be a constant hurdle. It takes time to relearn everything, until one day when you realise you have become part of your new community, an Aussie like any other.

In my case, the more I learned the more I wanted to know even more about this beautiful land. Shortcomings came my way in abundance as well, but I've learned to take them in my stride and embraced the culture. Having "a fair go" led me undoubtedly to wonderful new adventures and new stories to tell. Sometimes you get it right on your first attempt, sometimes you don't, and you try again, and again. That is all you can do.

It's like learning how to drive a car: when you first hop in a car and the driving instructor tells you "Let's go!", if you are like me, you wouldn't know what to do. You need to apply the process: adjust your seat, rear mirror, put on your safety belt, start the engine, put the signal on and so on. It may feel daunting if you haven't done it before. But then your brain adjusts slowly, and you learn how to navigate to the point of doing it without thinking. The muscle memory sets in. You are happy then. You can do it! And then another day comes and, as you've been driving comfortably on the right-hand side of the road, you arrive in a country where the whole traffic goes on the left-hand side. Terrifying at first. At least, that was my case. My stubborn brain and my eyes struggled to adjust when dealing with the incoming traffic. It took me a while, but I got there, with a little push and pull, and lots of perseverance. My poor local driving instructor, he learned a few words from me alright, when I was taking a wrong turn, a great experience exchange! We learned from each other.

Over time, my inquisitorial mind led me to reading more about Australia's history. "Such a young nation" I thought, in comparison to some other countries in the world. Yet, upon reflection, I arrived at the conclusion that there was much more to study about it, by including its old traditions and sacred places, which existed way beyond the initial landing of Captain James Cook's "HMS Endeavour" at Kernell, on Botany Bay shores in 1770.

A "through and through" Aussie once told me "You can't consider yourself a real Aussie unless you have visited Uluru at least once." So, I wondered: "What is Uluru?"

It sparked my imagination and insatiable curiosity to the point where, one day, my husband, Mike, and I, decided to visit this enigmatic place, in the heart of Northern Territory, about 450km from Alice Springs. It used to be called Ayers Rock, until Eddie Koiki

Mabo, an Indigenous Australian man from the Torres Strait Islands, known for his role in campaigning for Indigenous land rights in Australia, managed to win a Supreme Court decision and claimed it back for the Indigenous people, the land they and their ancestors had lived on for thousands of years.

Uluru is a sacred site, a large sandstone formation in the centre of Australia. But it is much more than that. According to the local Aboriginal people, called Anangu, Uluru's numerous caves and fissures were formed by ancestral beings during the Dreaming. They still hold ceremonies there to this day.

The Dreaming or Dreamtime is a term that refers to a cultural view attributed to Australian Aboriginal beliefs.

One of the main narratives associated with Uluru according to mainstream media, is about the Mala people. The Mala, who came from the North, decided one day to spend some time at Uluru to perform a special ceremony. Two men from another tribe, Wintalka, coming from the West, invited the Mala people to attend their own ceremony, but the Mala declined their invitation.

When the two Wintalka men returned to their tribe and told them what happened, the story goes that the Wintalka people got angry and created an evil spirit that took the form of a giant devil-dog who they ordered to go and destroy the Mala. Although the Mala were warned by a kingfisher woman about the danger coming their way, they did not believe her. So, the devil-dog, transformed into a ghost at this stage, attacked and killed some of the men, and the other Mala people fled to the South, towards what is now known as the state of South Australia.

The Anangu people, the traditional owners of Uluru sacred land, believe that they are the direct descendants of these ancestral beings who had created this landscape many thousands of years ago, and see it as a resting place for ancient spirits.

With all this info on the back of our minds, one October day in 2022, Mike and I booked a flight from Sydney to Alice Springs, at the beginning of spring. On arrival we hired a car. A short drive to the hotel and we settled in for the night at Crown Plaza Resort. Beautiful weather, great surroundings, it seemed like a perfect start for a new adventure. Just like we liked it.

The following morning, we had an early breakfast and without further ado, we jumped in the hire car and off we went. We figured the 450 km drive to Uluru would be easy, and we were keen to get there sooner rather than later. Maybe we should have factored in a few more other things.

For example, that as nice as the tarred road was, with some light or no traffic at all, the landscape was all but barren all the way. And we still needed to stop from time to time for short breaks, right? It was so much "nothingness", meaning no manmade structures to be seen whichever way you looked, that I felt like we entered another world's dimension. I hadn't seen anything like that before in my life. After a while, my eyes started to play games on me. I thought I was seeing settlements coming up on the horizon, with red roofs and dusty chimneys, but there was nothing but some sporadic bushes and red dirt as far as I could see in any direction. Sometimes a few random trees popped up from the arid terrain. Other times I thought I could see people walking on the side of the road, but there was nobody. The only movement on the ground came from some scattered herds of cows, grazing on their own, in that vast domain. "Hmmm" I said to myself after a while, "There is literally no human soul in sight," as I was glancing at those unanimated flood warning posts guarding the road.

After our first hundred kilometres, we started looking for a resting area, to have some coffee and stretch our legs. There was none. Only continuous dry land. "Bugger!" I grumbled.

After another hundred kilometres we were getting a bit anxious to find a petrol pump. Luckily enough we saw a signpost showing that it was coming up in another 80km. Great! A long way to find a petrol station in this unwavering territory. Eventually, we arrived at the Shell Uluru/Ayers Rock Service station and filled up the tank. "Ah! What a relief" I sighed. Mike pointed out the price. Whatever you think you would normally pay for your petrol anywhere in Australia, make sure you double it. A price to remember. In the middle of nowhere, who can argue with the price?!

A quick cup of coffee and a biscuit, and we were back on the road.

The route winded a few times, and after one of these turns, we saw this big top flat formation on the horizon. "Uluru!" we shouted in unison. We decided to take a break and stopped at the cattle station, called Curtin Springs, that unexpectedly came up, and we snapped a few photos. The nice lady at the coffee shop following our enthusiasm clarified the confusion. "You're looking at Mount Conner, not Uluru. Different shape and colours," she added. "Alright, thank you, we learned something new today," I replied politely, slightly embarrassed.

After about another one-and-a-half-hour drive, we could finally see the Uluru monolith in the distance. Intertwined pallets of dark green, gold, and brown bushes on an open canvas, stretching towards a spectacular huge red rock standing tall on the horizon, captured our undivided attention. We stopped on the dirt side lane and took a few photos from afar, admiring the view. "Fascinating!" I exclaimed.

We hit the road again and shortly entered the Uluru Kata Tjuta National Park area. Ten minutes later we arrived at the Cultural Centre, a locally made mud brick structure, designed by Anangu, park staff and architects, in the shape of two ancestral snakes. Local artists expressed themselves in numerous paintings, ceramics, glass, and wood, telling the story of their people.

Another cold soft drink in the visitors' lounge area, and our journey continued to its last loop, the parking lot, just a few kilometres away.

As we got out of the car and approached the Uluru site on foot, the atmosphere turned slightly eerie. There were a few people around, chatting in a deep voice only metres away, and still, I could not hear anything else but the quiet.

By now it was a beautiful warm afternoon. Few clouds in the sky but nothing to worry about. Or so we thought.

And there it was, Uluru, standing 348 metres high, and with a 9.4 km circumference, as the brochure asserted. Impressive!

A breathtaking site for any visitor who lays eyes on it for the first time. I was in awe at its massive scale and ever-changing colours from deeply red to purple and to orange, as I learned, depending on the angle of the sunlight and the time of day, and I remembered that climbing Uluru, once a popular touristic attraction, has been forbidden since 2019 out of respect for the traditional landowners' spiritual significance as well as for ensuring safety measures for enthusiastic hikers.

The closer I walked towards the rock, the more I felt a connection of sorts with the place. Hard to explain.

"Hey, darl" I asked my husband, "What do you think?"

Mike uttered: "It's amazing, isn't it?" I nodded in agreement.

We took the base walk around the monolith and moved closer to its caves, crevasses, and waterholes. Deafening silence. As I stood there for a minute or so to take it all in, I felt like the wind was somehow intending to speak to me. I fluttered.

"Can you hear the wind soothing through the leaves of the trees?" I asked Mike.

"Not sure if it's just the wind or it's something else..." he answered.

"What do you mean?" I insisted.

"It may seem weird, but I felt like a chill was running up my back," he replied with a slight shiver. "Don't laugh," he teased me.

"Who's laughing?" I mumbled. I shut my eyes, stood still and really focused on listening to the breeze. It resonated with me, as in a kind of deep-down energy flow. I couldn't explain it, I could just feel that there was something there in the air.

"I think I know what you mean," I murmured.

Mike looked up at the sides of the monolith and pointed to the caves and the Aboriginal drawings. "Wow, this is really something!

These paintings have been around for at least 30,000 years, as the literature says!" Following the direction of Mike's hand, I noticed the beautiful rock art. "This is really something special," I contemplated. "You get a sense of awe, thinking that people have been living around this area for thousands of years."

We continued to follow the walking track until we came about a small observation area, with a spectacular view of the various facets of the rock.

Mike turned towards me and said in a low voice, "Let's just sit down here on this bench, near the little plaque 'The quiet spot' ". So, we did. We rested on the bench, closed our eyes, holding hands, and listened. "An out of this world experience," I sensed. The wind hugged us, and ushered through the leaves around us, vibrating in sync with our thoughts. I allowed myself to be carried away for a few moments. It was like I was being welcomed by an invisible warmth of this sacred place. Thoughts of joy and utmost happiness were going through my mind in a flash, as if it were years. I was amazed. That spiritual experience stayed with me for more than ten minutes. Almost like a meditation experience. I didn't want it to go away. The message was simple, yet so powerful: "All is good!" That's it, that's all I received in that unique moment. I waited there for a couple more minutes. I could hear Mike's breath near me, and then slowly I opened my eyes.

"Wow!" I said, as he was examining my face." Did you feel that?" I blurted.

"Yes, I did," he answered.

"Incredible!" I exclaimed. "Absolutely beautiful!" he echoed.

We continued our walk around the rock in silence, following the bending walkway. Then we took a side path towards some caves, and we stopped, admiring the artistry on the walls. They say that Uluru started to form about 550 million years ago, which makes it 250 million years older than the dinosaurs! Which is why it's thought to be one of the oldest rocks on the planet. Imagine how much these walls could tell if they could speak.

We reached the end of the short touristic trail and stopped at the end, at the pond. You could see the deep dark brown vertical marks encrusted on the sandstone and imagine the torrents of water shooting down with a vengeance for thousands of years on heavy rainy days. Yet, there it was, a crystal-clear water pool at the bottom.

I came close to the rim of its landing area and looked down at my reflection. Few ripples transited swiftly although the wind had stopped. I gasped. It was happening again. That message came to my mind, clearly speaking to me "It's all good, don't worry." I checked around cautiously. Complete silence.

Mike was waiting for me patiently in the alley. I said goodbye to my newfound "spiritual friend," the pond, and I strolled away, still holding in that great feeling of calmness and absolute serenity.

We chatted for a while and then, deep in thought, we made our way back to the car. A few sporadic rain droplets started to splash around, and the wind picked up a notch. A storm was coming.

It's been only 3 hours since we descended on this fabulous Indigenous land, but it felt like we have been there for far longer than that. A strong connection to this site has formed inside me, and it was there to stay. I wished we had more time, but soon it was going to be dark, and we needed to return to Alice Springs. "Only another five and a half hours drive," I thought to myself slightly displeased.

We managed to reach our car just in time. The sky has turned into dark grey shades and the wind switched gears to a blasting level, threatening to engulf us all in a whirlpool of dust.

We left in a hurry and kept quiet in the car for a while. At the junction, we took a last glimpse at this fantastic site that startled our imagination as we were exiting the National Park. We glanced at each other, and we understood. One day we will return. No words were spoken, no need, this promise was just for us to keep.

The dark night started to creep in as we turned our beams on. No soul around.

By the time we reached the Petrol station, the same one as on our way in, and we filled up the car, the store assistant told us that we had arrived just in time. The Petrol station was closing for the night. "What a relief!" I exhaled.

"Some local Aboriginal elders had passed by earlier today, and they predicted a heavy rain coming up tonight," she added. "Be careful! You shouldn't be driving late at night around here. It's dangerous!" the store assistant expressed worryingly.

"We'll be fine, thanks!" Mike dismissed the warning with a wave.

We left the Petrol station and ventured into the pitch-black night. No lights in sight, no stars, no cars, nothing but the road and us. Spooky!

Big raindrops started to pound the car's top. The visibility was poor, so Mike reduced the speed as a precaution. I could not see anything around us but that little stretch of road ahead of us, with the flood warning poles soldering on, lit by the car beams. They reminded me of their intended purpose: "I hope we don't end up in a flood zone," I worried.

Two hours passed and my eyes grew increasingly fatigued by constantly gazing at the road. Mike and I kept talking for a while to stay awake, but at some point, we both started yawning uncontrollably. "What to do?" I wondered. Almost like reading my mind, Mike answered my unasked question: "Not much we can do, we need to keep going!"

Eventually, despite my defiance, I started dozing on and off, when, all of a sudden, I heard this message taking shape in my mind "Stop!" I wasn't sure where it came from or if it was just a dream, but the call became louder and louder until I cried out loud without thinking "Stop the car!"

Mike stared at me perplexedly and asked "Why? What's going on?"

"Stop the car. Now!!," I screamed with conviction. He hit the brakes abruptly, alarmed by my reaction.

The car came to a halt with a screech. We saw nothing ahead, except for the heavy downpour of rain, and the constant beat of the windscreen wipers, working overtime. Or so we thought. By now the visibility was down to less than fifty metres, the poor wipers barely clearing a way through the rainfall.

Then suddenly, we noticed a sea of eyes, staring at us in the dark. Scary! At closer inspection we detected a herd of cattle standing there, blocking the road right in front of us, brightened by an errant lightning flash, which temporarily lit up the skyline in front of our stationary car. We leaned in closer to the car windscreen, like a couple of short-sighted people trying to peer through the fogged-up glass. They looked like a shadowy groundswell, hanging in there, undisturbed by the rain or by the lights or by anything else for that matter.

We would have crashed straight into them if that little voice in my head hadn't fired up. "Phew!" I spewed, "That was a scare!"

Mike was flabbergasted. "How did you know?" he asked.

"I didn't", I replied, "It was just this instant warning in my head."

Mike and I looked at each other in disbelief for a few tense moments.

"What now?", I muttered.

"No idea," he responded. "They don't seem to want to move aside!"

"So, when in doubt, what do you do when you get stuck, and you don't know what else to do?" I questioned myself. "You google it!"

I grabbed my phone in my bag. "Great, we have a signal!" I marvelled and hit the search engine in a rush, typing questions: How do you move stationary cattle from a road? How to safely move cattle? What equipment is used to move cattle? What movement should be used to move cattle in a field?

Big-city people as we were, we didn't have much freelance exposure to farm animal encounters. Soon we worked it out that we needed a stick, but we had none of that and the side lane was barren. At a glance, the umbrella stashed in the trunk appeared to be a good substitute. The safety measures read that you were not supposed to get out of the car when encountering a herd of any kind of animals, but that was not an option, as the cattle could have been standing there all night and we had somewhere else to be. We ruled it out. And the direction instruction, as in which direction you should approach a herd if you want them to follow your lead, apparently walking in the opposite direction of the direction of the desired movement was the way to go. Unfortunately, that didn't apply here either, as the cattle were standing right there in the middle of the road, with no indication of where they wanted to go. So, it was a simple case of "take your pick."

Once we finished with the situational risk analysis, we decided that Mike would go round the back of the car and fetch the umbrella, while I jump in the driver's seat and keep the engine going with both wipers and beams turned on.

Said and done. Mike hopped out and picked up the brolly by which time he was already soaked. In a frenzy, he started swinging his makeshift sword up in the air like a warrior, in a brave attempt to drive them away from the right side to the left side of the road. When that didn't work, he switched flanks and tried the other way, cheering them up. It took a few long couple of minutes until the sleepy cows appeared to get the message and started ambling slowly out of the way, pushing each other's back reluctantly, to the right.

"Victory!", Mike shouted, and hurried back in the car, drenched to the bone. The wet trail followed him inside, the water dripping on the floor. "You look like you'd taken a shower and forgot to take your clothes off," I laughed. "Righto," he giggled, wiping his face. "Next time you do it, smarty pants!" We both chuckled.

As our good spirits returned, we fastened our seat belts, and I began to drive carefully, until some flickers of lights surfaced in the far distance.

"Alice Springs!" Mike exclaimed.

"At last!" I agreed.

It was just over 10.00pm when we reached the hotel. I parked the car, we picked up our belongings and we made our way to the room, scampering around the potholes, feeling exhausted but content. That day's trip felt like a terrific achievement of an introspection of sorts, a journey into self-reflection and no pretence.

We ordered room service and enjoyed our return to civilisation. A hot shower and I was ready to go to bed, while Mike was lingering a little longer on the sheltered balcony, a cigarette in his hand, listening to the drumming down rain.

As I was lying in bed, thinking of what we had experienced that day, I felt like this gentle, warm night breeze was embracing me, while the "All is good" whispers persisted in my ears.

Mike returned to the bedroom, switched off the lights and hugged me lovingly. "One day we will return to Uluru, that is a promise", he mumbled. I agreed with him in my mind and contentedly drifted into a well-deserved deep sleep.

Second Chance at Friendship

A gripping tale of a long-awaited encounter between two estranged friends.

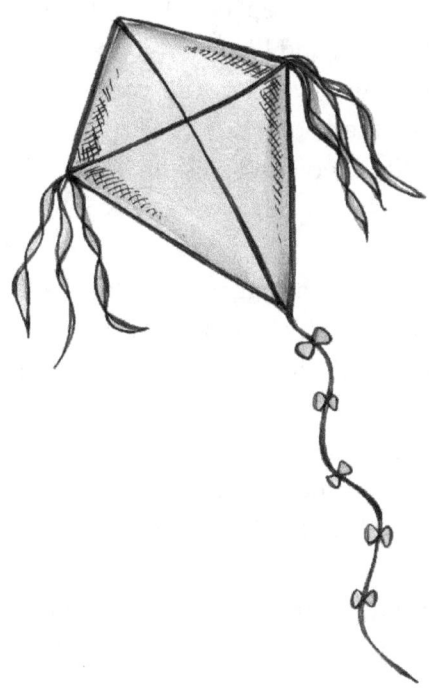

One cold October evening I was enjoying a cup of tea with my husband Mike, chilling on the coach in front of the TV, watching a movie on Netflix in our cosy Watsons Bay apartment, in Sydney, when out of the blue I received a WhatsApp call. I usually don't take calls if I don't recognise the number, but somehow on this occasion, I decided to pick it up, not knowing what to expect.

"Hello Julia," a slightly hesitant voice called my name. "This is Mia. I'm not sure if you still remember me", the voice continued.

"Mia," I exclaimed in disbelief. My heart started racing. I couldn't believe it was her; I was speechless.

"Are you there?" she checked cautiously.

"Yes, what a pleasant surprise!" I finally snapped out of it and replied in autopilot mode. "How did you find me?" I queried.

"Our old friend Alex passed me your number," she explained.

"I'm so glad he did," I sighed. "How have you been?"

"I'm good, thanks", she replied," Look, I'm coming to Perth for a conference next month, and I have an 8-hour stopover in Sydney, on the return leg, and I was wondering if you would like to meet, if you are available", she asked politely.

"Absolutely, Mia! I wouldn't miss it in the world! I can't wait to see you", I confirmed.

"How about we meet at Circular Quay if that's OK? I would like to see the Opera House!" she suggested. "The architect in me wouldn't want to miss an opportunity like this to marvel at its grandeur."

"Done," I committed on the spot and quickly worked out the details.

We ended the call.

"Mia is coming to Sydney, amazing!" I burst out with excitement.

"Who was that darling?" Mike enquired, puzzled by my spontaneous reaction.

"A good old friend of mine, Mia, from back in the day in my uni years," I replied, distracted by a sudden flashback.

"Who is Mia? I haven't heard you talking about her before", he pressed on.

"It's a long story," I replied with a sigh.

"I would like to hear it," he continued, "If you'd like to talk about it."

"Sure, why not?" I agreed, taken back by his genuine curiosity. "It was an interesting chapter of my life, long before I met you."

"I'm all ears," said Mike, lounging comfortably on the couch, switching off the TV.

"Many years ago," I started my recount," I was on my way to completing my engineering degree while taking part in a vocal group of enthusiasts who practiced choir songs. I loved the singing."

"I know that much," he joked. "Please continue."

"Mia was my good friend at the time, and she was studying Architectural Design, but music was our shared passion. Initially there wasn't much interaction between us other than the singing part and the usual rehearsal chatter. I was a couple of years older than her, and we were born in different cities, hundreds of kilometres away from each other. I was from Bucharest, Romania, as you know, and she was from Brasov. We became close over time when we discovered that we held similar values and overall life interests, apart from singing. The more we talked the more we felt connected to each other at a deep kind of level."

I recollected my memories and continued "Mia was a bright student, always studying hard. Since an early age she had a clear goal, to complete a PhD in Architectural Design. Not many students I knew, including myself, were interested in getting down that pathway of an ultimate intellectual challenge. But Mia was different. She wanted to prove herself and upheld this utmost desire to make a difference in the world. I admired her commitment. She was determined to do anything in her power to achieve her goal despite the personal sacrifices that came with it. No valuable deed comes for free."

I took a sip of my tea and continued uninterrupted, "As for myself, even if I enjoyed studying for the most part, that engineering degree in steel works wasn't exactly something I was prepared to pursue to the moon and back. I think I mentioned this to you before. I liked some elements of it, such as the special mathematics subject (pretty odd choice one could say!!). However, if I am to be completely honest, working with metals was far from being what some would say "a call" for me. I accepted it and followed it through, as a duty. At least it helped me secure a good job in a large plant and what was considered at the time a good pay, but that was where it ended. It served its purpose.

"I remember you telling me about that, I always admired your maths skills," said Mike, dimming the ceiling lights.

"My genuine passion was music though," I pressed on with my story, "I really loved that experience of learning how to sing. It was my first long-term goal I have ever had, that came as a package with the buzz ensued by performing on stage in front of hundreds of people, such an adrenaline rush. You could say it was also a hobby, since I was doing it in my own spare time, trying to develop my artistic skills, while studying to become a steel engineer, a very different career direction. However, pursuing my passion came at a cost. To keep it going and be allowed to participate in the artistic events, music festivals and associated rehearsals, I had to maintain high-level grades for all my exams. That was the deal I had made with my parents. They wanted me to have a "proper job," like a steel engineer, following in my father's shoes. The music in their eyes was taking me "nowhere." But I wanted both, and I knew I could pull it off. I was certainly not prepared to give up the music. So, my parents and I kept our side of the bargain and it worked. At least for a while. They were educated people who enjoyed going to theatre and opera shows occasionally and sometimes to odd classical music concerts. Since they thought my choir singing was a waste of time, they treated it with minimal interest. I was conflicted at times, "Should I pursue singing or engineering?" Not knowing which one to choose I persisted in both for a while.

"I can totally understand your dilemma," Mark conceded tenderly.

I returned to my storyline acknowledging his remark, "The music shows meant the world to me. That artistic lifestyle I was living played an important role in my personal development and transitioning to adulthood. My mum made an effort a couple of times and attended my shows. It was good to know she was there for me in the audience. My father never came. He was busy with work; you remember what he was like!" Mike gave an affirming nod, and motion with his hand for me to continue." So, I perfected my singing performance and delved into the showbiz industry intricacies, while I was studying hard to achieve my degree, as per my family request."

I paused for a few moments to catch my breath. Mike was listening to me in silence.

"My friend Mia had a different upbringing than mine," I continued, "At least this was my understanding. Her parents were pretty much into music, book writing and arts, so her interest in arts peaked early on in her life. Expressing herself through music was a blessing, something that came from the heart that needed to be shared.

I didn't know much about Mia's personal life in the beginning, our chats were mainly focused on the songs we were learning and rehearsing together with the group, three times per week. Both of us were sopranos, so being able to achieve a high pitch and sustain it as long as it was required was very important to us. We both wanted to excel at our part, competing with the others and trying to achieve perfection. During breaks we used to hide away in the ladies' room to perform scales and to listen to our trills. The bathroom had the best acoustics, of course. We encouraged each other to go again and again and provided feedback on the tone, tempo, and voice projection. We wanted to be the best. A nice and genuine bond formed over time. The beauty of it was that we weren't even aware of it. However, it helped us understand how to attack a new music sheet with confidence, how to reach a high note and how to breathe properly, as it was expected of us."

I took another sip and pressed on, "Months passed by, and our friendship grew stronger. Gradually, we opened up to each other as we gained more trust in our abilities, and we started asking questions about our dreams, as in where we wanted to be in our life in a distant future. We both felt we didn't fit in with the communist Romania dogmatic regime, but we never came up with an alternative solution. We didn't rule it out either, it was just a blank canvas."

"Hmmm. Tough times," he contemplated upon my words.

"I was so focused on the music that I didn't even ask Mia about her specific studies in design," I proceeded, "Although I knew she was passing her exams with flying colours. I made a point to congratulate her every time she brought it up, when she achieved another High Distinction, which was quite often to be honest. It was inspiring to know someone like her, so determined to study and achieve her full academic potential."

"How was Mia as a person?" Mike inquired.

"She had a great personality," I replied, picturing her in my mind.

"She was friendly, trustworthy, funny, gentle, sometimes quiet, but always very pleasant to talk to. Plus, she was a deep thinker, which was a big tick for me. A woman of substance would have been my description of her. Still is to this day."

"She sounds like a lovely person. I would like to meet her," Mike concluded. "Please continue."

"As I was approaching my final study year, I took an interest in journalism and started writing articles for a local university newspaper. It offered me a different exploration angle, meeting with other students and learning about their lives, struggles and achievements. I even had a mentor for a short while who guided me through the art of writing. I enjoyed it. He was great. Unfortunately, he was always busy, until our time together fizzled out."

"I didn't know you were a journo," Mike exclaimed in surprise.

"I gave it a crack, a long time ago," I tittered.

"You should do it again; it sounds like you were quite fond of it. Anyway, back to Mia please," he kept me on point.

"One day I decided to write about Mia," I carried on, "As a brand-new reporter, I was happy to be able to offer her a level of exposure for her research. We sat down in a quiet uni corner, and we talked. And then we talked some more. Doing that interview was exciting, especially when I realised that even so early in her career Mia was already so knowledgeable. I asked questions, listened to her, and I took notes. The article was well received. Students felt inspired by one of their own and wondered how she had time to do all that work in such a short time. My editor gave me a pat on the back, "Well done, Julia." It felt good. Her tremendous efforts were being acknowledged, tick. "

"Well done darling," said Mike. "That was a nice touch."

"Last time I met Mia, 30 years ago, hint, hint", I resumed, "I was at a pop concert, by chance. I still remember dancing and jumping around in a frenzy, in tune with the rhythms on stage. Michael Jackson's concert. Say no more. We sang and danced along full of enthusiasm. Happy times."

"30 years", Mark pondered.

At this point, I took a break to finish my cup of tea. He was waiting for me patiently to resume my narrative.

"So, what happened next?" he inquired after a few minutes.

"Well, life happened," I added with a smile. "Once I graduated, I had to relocate to a new city to start my employment far away from my home, folks, and friends. My life changed in an instant when I entered the "real world stage" to make a living.

As a 23-year-old ambitious young lady in a male-dominated industry, I faced challenges every step of the way, so "trial and error" became my new "go to" strategy."

"I remember that bit. You told me before. That must have been tough," he acknowledged.

"Yes, it was," I admitted, "The distance, and the lack of interaction with my loved ones took a toll on me. I missed my buddies, the rehearsals, my family. And I lost contact with Mia entirely. I felt bad that I didn't have a chance to tell her how much her friendship meant to me."

"You shouldn't beat yourself up on this, these things happen," he empathised with me.

"New emergencies took over my life, they required my full attention, "I confessed" To find a place to live and to navigate the new world of being a young employee at a plant that started shifts at 6.00am every morning, were just a few. Massive changes to my previous lifestyle choices came into play and working late hours to earn money and support myself having no one to turn to, did my head in. Luckily enough my survival instincts kicked in. But I missed Mia, a lot," I finally concluded my story.

We kept quiet for a few minutes, deep in thought.

"I love you so much," said Mike, leaning towards me and giving me a kiss. "You've been through so much."

"I love you too," I replied, and gave him a hug.

By now it was getting late, time to go to bed.

Three weeks later and the moment of truth was approaching fast. The night before my reunion with Mia I couldn't sleep much. I checked my face wrinkles in the bathroom's mirror wondering, "How much have I changed? Would she recognise me? I mean it's been 30 years!! No one escapes the passing of time."

Finally, the day of our meeting has arrived. I was so excited. "Enjoy!" Mike wished me on my way out.

I jumped on the train to Martin Place without delay and took a vigorous walk down to Circular Quay. I didn't want to be late. We haven't seen each other for so long, nor have we ever been in contact in any way. "Would we still be able to connect?" I wondered. "No point in worrying," I encouraged myself.

At 7.30am sharp I arrived at Wharf 5, at Circular Quay, our meeting point, and scrutinised the platform in all directions, anxiously.

And there she was, beautiful Mia, standing right there in front of me on the pavement. She sported some black jeans with a fancy dark green jacket. A small black carry-on bag was resting in an upright position beside her hip. Her deep dark brown eyes were contrasting with her blond curly hair. She smiled at me. Yes, she had put on a few kilos, but she looked great.

"Mia," I said in a loving voice, throwing my arms around her.

"Julia," she replied, mirroring my warm welcome reaction.

We hugged a few times in astonishment.

Not many people ventured around the quay at that early hour, so I allowed myself to get carried away more than usual. Tears of joy formed in my eyes, but I bravely held them in. This encounter was really happening!

"OMG, you're here!", I cried. "We managed to meet in flesh and blood, although we are living worlds apart. How have you been? Tell me all about you, I want to know everything," I pressed on.

"I live in the US now, Texas," she said. "My life has been crazy, but it's all good! Where should I start?" she answered.

"Come on, out with it, I can't wait," I exclaimed with excitement.

The conversation warmed up quickly, so many things to share. First, she warned me that she didn't have a chance to sleep much the previous night as she caught the red eye flight from Perth to Sydney, after the conference. But she was determined to make the most of our day together.

We snapped a few pictures with the Harbour Bridge behind us and looked around for a café to have breakfast and a coffee.

We sat down at City Extra Café, next to the train station entrance, and placed our order. A quick Espresso shot for Mia, to help her stay sharp, before food arrived.

All of a sudden, a bunch of colourful rosellas landed on our table. They stole a sugar sachet from a teacup plate and started ingesting the sweet granules with a vengeance. They looked like two good buddies, chirping happily, sharing their food. Mia took some snapshots, amused. "They look like us," I exclaimed, "Chatting away, sharing stories and having a meal". I laughed.

A familiar tune started playing on the speakers which I recognised instantly, but I held back, anticipating Mia's reaction.

"Isn't this the song we used to sing with the choir back in the day?" she recalled," It's Barbra Streisand's "Memory", isn't it?"

I nodded, trapped in a flashback. "What are the odds of listening to this song here, now?" I contemplated.

Mia started humming along with the melody in a faint voice; I followed her lead, surprised that I could still remember the lines.

When the song ended, we recomposed ourselves and finished our meal in silence.

It was like we picked up where we left it 30 years ago. We started walking slowly around the quay towards the Opera House, chit chatting away. There was no awkwardness, no tension, no pretence, just two old friends reunited, sharing from the heart.

The sun was trying hard to show its face from the clouds blocking its view; it was such a beautiful morning.

Mia signalled she was ready to take me back on her life journey.

"So, are you ready? Strap in!" she asked.

"From the beginning please," I replied waiting impatiently.

"Well, since I last saw you," she began, "Things had moved very quickly in my career, even before my graduation. One of my uni teachers informed me about a PhD opportunity that had come up at a university in Texas, USA, which was right down my alley of Architectural Design. He thought I would have a good chance to be accepted and I could advance my career should I choose to go down that pathway. So, I applied for it and guess what? I got it! I was over the moon. You know, these opportunities don't come up easy", she added.

"Good on you Mia! I always knew you were on to something big!", I exploded in admiration.

"I booked my flights and sorted out the accommodation in a week, and then it hit me. I was saying goodbye to my family, my fiancée, and my country, and I was starting a brand-new life on my own somewhere else. Even so, I felt like it was still a proposition I couldn't refuse", she disclosed.

She paused for a few moments to organise her thoughts.

"I was very close to Mum, it was hard to leave home," she recalled. "But I had decided that it was the right choice for me, to leap into the unknown and give it a go."

"I can totally relate to that," I echoed. "My mother found it very hard to let go of me too when my family and I decided to move to Australia. Please continue," I asked.

"The beginning was difficult," Mia kept going, "but I stayed focused on what was important, making it work for me, despite the hardships. At times, I wasn't sure if I could make it, but I stuck to my guns and stayed put, and resumed my research."

"I know what you mean," I interrupted her, "As a migrant, I always felt pulled at times between the two worlds. The one I left behind with which I still had some ties to and the new world where I needed to learn to survive quickly and keep my eyes on the ball so to speak."

"That's right," she agreed." And then, you see, my fiancée was waiting for me back home in Romania. So, I had to make a decision. To follow my dream or to go back. I initially thought I could do both. But things got in the way. Sometimes it is just not meant to be. All those questions swirling through my mind, the "what ifs," the doubts... I wish I had a magic wand to tell me what to do," she said in a melancholic but steady voice.

"That must have been tough for you," I empathised.

"Yes, it was," she confirmed.

"The only thing you can do though when you feel you're going down the rabbit hole is to keep going," I added, "At least that's what I learned".

"I couldn't agree more", she replied. "From there onwards my career took off. I completed my PhD and secured a professor role at the same university. Mum was so happy and proud of me," she chuckled, "And yet, she couldn't accept that I was not going back. Things had changed." She paused to gather her thoughts.

"When my father passed away the whole situation became even more complicated. Especially when mum's health deteriorated, as she was living by herself, not knowing what to do anymore. I tried to help as much as I could, I took some time off to be with her, but it was hard," she acknowledged.

"And then, when I was appointed Chief Architect of a large-scale project in Dallas, I threw myself into my work with everything I've got. I was going to create this massive cutting-edge design of a building project and embed the latest sustainability features to protect the environment. Everything I had been working for up to that stage was coming into play. A wonderful but challenging initiative." Her eyes were sparkling.

Listening to her storyline I felt inspired like back in the day when I was conducting my first interview with Mia.

"Did you miss home?" I asked.

"Oh, yes," she answered." I longed for my hometown, Brasov, where I grew up and had a happy childhood. However, over time I knew I had arrived at a different but good place for me. I evolved into a completely new person, hardwired to my new community, where I felt appreciated, and where I could contribute."

"How about your singing passion? What happened with that?" I asked.

She chuckled. "Nothing that some visits to museums and going to concerts couldn't fix. They filled in the gap. I was too busy working…What about you? Are you still singing?" she returned the question.

"Neah," I replied." I joined a Sydney choir once, but it didn't work out. It wasn't the same. They weren't rehearsing enough, at least not to the level I was used to, I didn't like it. So, I found refuge in the musical theatre shows coming to Sydney every season, close enough to what you're doing", I concluded.

"What about you Julia?" Mia asked. "How did you decide to come to Australia? What happened with your engineering career?"

"A long story short," I said, "Moving to Australia wasn't initially in the cards, ha, ha. Unlike you, my engineering career didn't quite do it for me in the long run, although I gave it 9 years of my life. I experimented with other industries, free zones, mergers and acquisitions, banking, just to name a few. I was looking for something meaningful and fulfilling."

"So, what did you do?" she enquired.

"Well, as it happened, I met a wonderful man, Mike. We hit it off although we had very different upbringing. We got married and had a beautiful daughter, Carla. Here, I'll show you some photos", I said, grabbing my phone from my purse. Mia scrolled down through some photos for a few seconds and said, "How nice. You are a lucky girl Julia" and smiled candidly.

"For many years I thought we were set for life in that new lifestyle environment after communism fell," I continued" But the stars had other plans for us." I paused for a while to catch my breath.

"One day, Carla, our daughter, expressed her utmost desire to study overseas if she was given the chance to become a solicitor of international law. She wanted to make the world a better place. She was only 12 years old. Go figure," I resumed.

"No way!" exclaimed Mia. I nodded and continued "We took the democratic approach, and held a brief family unit deliberation, and decided to sell up, pack up and move on to Australia."

"By then my parents had passed away, my friends were too busy to notice what was going on, and it just felt the right thing to do. Australia, my husband's country of birth, stood for all the right values we resonated with, and we wanted to be part of," I explained.

"Now, that is an interesting twist," Mia pondered.

"Should I continue?" I enquired.

"Absolutely, please go on," she replied enthusiastically.

"Learning how things were done in Oz land had its challenges. I didn't have much time for making new friends. I needed to find a job and to learn things, fast...," I stated.

"What did you find different here?" she wanted to know.

"Are you kidding?" I chuckled. "Walking on the left-hand side of the pedestrian pathway for starters took some serious adjustment, since all my life I was wired to follow the right-hand route. And then Christmas, ah! How can you have Christmas celebrations when outside it's 42 degrees Celsius? As you know, where we grew up, Christmas was usually "white," with lots of snow and freezing temperatures!?", I emotionally spit it out.

"So, what did you do?" she inquired.

"I adjusted slowly to the point where I have become an Aussie like any other, without even realising it. It was just a matter of applying myself, day by day, just like you did," I acknowledged with honesty.

"And I did something else too," I added. "Careerwise, I transitioned to education. Sharing my experience, knowledge, and skills with young adults eager to learn seemed to be the right thing to do. Moreover, I developed and carried out wellbeing workshops with people in need, trying to help them overcome their own hardships and focus on the bright side."

"Tell me more about that," she probed.

"Not much else to tell, really." I continued. "My freelance attempt didn't go far but it was rewarding while it lasted. My students were so happy; I kept their feedback forms to remind myself of why I'd done it. It made a difference, even if it was only on a small scale", I ended my story.

She kept quiet for a few moments, deep in thought.

We looped around the Opera House forecourts area, and stopped at the safety balustrade, taking in the views.

"Such a marvel!" she exclaimed in awe, gazing at the Opera House structure.

Suddenly a five or six-year-old girl passed by holding a thread to a big green and yellow flowery kite in her hand, chasing the wind. She interrupted our thoughts. She was determined to make it fly, but the sea breeze wouldn't pick up. She ran around in circles a couple of times to no avail. Then she went back to the building and sprinted towards the bay to catch a blow in her kite. We watched her struggle vaguely entertained and wondered what she was up to next.

Her mum was standing a few meters away, talking to some friends. From time to time, she turned around and alerted her child lovingly, "Monica, be careful! There are people around; please come back here." Little Monica though wouldn't give it up.

Her mum's efforts to keep her daughter at bay were in total contrast with the girl's disobedience.

"Does that remind you of someone we know?" I asked Mia cheekily.

"Yeah, yeah, I could say the same thing about you," landed her reply.

We were strolling around the forecourts by the ocean, until something caught my eye.

The little kite enthusiast had gone back to the Opera House walls and was preparing for a new brave launch. Something didn't sit quite well with me. By the time I opened my mouth to express my concern, Monica was flying by us, the string in her hand, staring at the kite, heading straight towards the bay.

She reached the safety rail right when the wind picked up the pace throwing her kite up in the air. Monica was so happy of her success, she swivelled on her feet and hailed at her mum, to show her the extraordinary achievement. Without warning the wind snatched the kite from her fingers and blew it over the balustrade. In a panic, she climbed the safety rail and tried to catch it, but the string eluded her grasp. She stretched her body upright, throwing her hands up in the air, aiming at the kite, and before I could react, she lost her balance and fell into the choppy waters below.

"Nooooo," I cried in unison with Mia, who was watching the action unfolding in front of our eyes worryingly.

It all happened so fast.

Hearing our desperate call, the mum and her friends turned around, wondering what happened.

Without a word, Mia and I raced to the balustrade as fast as we could and surveyed the water.

"There she is," I said, pointing out in her direction.

Monica was fighting for her life, clearly at risk of drowning. Knowing I couldn't swim I frantically searched around for anyone or anything that could help her.

Mia sprang into action without hesitation. She unzipped her jacket hurriedly and threw it on the ground, then took off her travel boots and handed her carry-on bag over to me. She climbed the rail confidently and off she plunged into the sea. I was watching in horror.

Monica's mother started screaming, finally comprehending the dire situation.

"Mia, hurry, I can't see her," I cried, clenching at the rail.

Mia took a first dive and came up empty. She went in again. And again.

At this point I noticed a water taxi headed to the bay not far from us and I started waving Mia's jacket up high, pleading for help.

Monica's mother suddenly understood the danger her daughter was in and started screaming for help in desperation, waving her arms with conviction. Her friends joined in our signalling efforts.

Finally, Mia managed to get a firm grip on the girl's summer dress and pulled her head out of the water, face up, supporting her in a holding pattern. The girl choked a few times and slowly regained her breath. Mia steadied her arm around her.

"At last," I exclaimed full of hope.

The water taxi chauffeur noticed the struggle and directed his boat towards the floating pair. The mum was hysterical by now, crying and yelling uncontrollably, "My baby, please save my baby!"

He stopped the boat near the little girl, and with Mia's help, pulled her onboard the water taxi, and signalled she was OK. Monica sat up a bit, leaning on a side, staring at her mum crying meters away on the quay, and wept candidly, "Mummy, I want my mummy."

Her mum kept repeating continuously, like in a trance, "Monica, Monica."

Mia climbed into the boat from the left side and the water taxi hurried to the docking point about one hundred metres down to the left, as per the rescuer's signs.

I picked up Mia's jacket and boots and rushed to the indicated pier, wheeling the carry-on bag behind me. A small crowd of people drawn by the unfolding incident followed in pursuit. I could see how the mum was finally comforting her child in her arms in a frenzy. Mia disembarked, soaked to the bone, but looked happy.

"Great job," the rescuer congratulated Mia with a captain's salute.

"It was nothing; you would have done the same for me," she replied in a humble voice, feeling shy of the attention rendered by the ad-hoc spectators who had exploded in frantic applauses, cheering at her.

"My goodness, you're amazing!" I said, and gave Mia a hug in admiration, still feeling jolted by the event.

We proceeded to check on the little girl. She seemed fine but clearly shaken, her mum trying to calm her down. She was holding her little treasure tight to her chest, not letting anyone come close to her. She was in total panic mode. One of her friends helped release Monica from her mum's protective arms, and assisted her with her breathing, in a calm voice. Slowly, her mum addressed her ravaged demeanour.

She walked towards us and, still slightly hyperventilating, introduced herself, "I'm Anna."

"Mia, and this is my friend Julia," Mia responded in kind.

"And this little cutie here is Monica," she continued in a gentle voice, holding Monica's shoulders lovingly.

"Thank you so much, Mia and Julia," she said, "You've been absolutely fantastic, I don't know what else to say, I can't even imagine what could have happened if you weren't here", she added and started sobbing, hiding her tears away from Monica.

"Thank you, Mia," the little girl echoed her mum in a shaky childlike voice, wrapped up in her mum's oversized pink jacket.

"Don't worry, Monica, everything will be just fine," Mia reassured the little girl and gave her a hug.

By now the paramedics had arrived. Straight away they focused their attention on Monica, checking for vitals, asking questions, and quickly concluded she was all right. No need to go to hospital. They covered her in a silver sheet to keep her warm and then talked to her mum, enquiring about what had happened.

With a nod, Mia assured them she was OK too, so they left her alone.

We waved at the taxi driver and went downstairs to the Opera House facilities, to give Mia a chance to change her wet clothes.

She returned in no time wearing jeans and a white T-shirt, her frizzy blond hair almost dry.

"The carry-on bag came in handy for such an unexpected event," I joked. "Weren't you afraid to jump in the ocean like that?" I asked.

She chuckled. "I do six laps in the pool every morning back home, before work. I like it," she replied with a wink.

"My Goodness is there anything you can't do?" I teased. "Don't answer that."

"Julia," continued Mia, "Next year I'm coming back to Australia for a Conference in Brisbane. We should meet."

"Absolutely!" I endorsed her suggestion with excitement.

"No excuses!" we continued in unison, bursting into laughter.

"You must promise me that you'll take a week off and come and stay with us in Sydney. I would love you to meet my family and I'll show you some nice places too. You MUST!" I proclaimed.

"Deal," she confirmed, "We cannot afford to miss out on our second chance at friendship."

Tears rolled down my face when we hugged goodbye. I didn't try to stop them this time. Hers fell on my shoulder. Emotions had been running high all morning, but now it was time to let go. Nostalgia set in.

I waited until she disappeared on the platform to the airport, veering her small black carry-on bag, and I started strolling back to Martin Place station deep in thought. "Real friends are so hard to find," I proclaimed to myself.

As I was waiting for my train, my phone beeped. It was Mia.

"Hey," she said in an emotional voice, "There is something I never told anyone, but I think you should know. When I was little, I had a younger sister, Sara. We used to play together every day. We had a nice backyard with a pool." She took a deep breath and continued choking a bit "One day when our parents went out for food shopping around the corner, Sara and I went outside to play as per usual, and as it was getting hot, I went inside to bring some ice-cream. By the time I came back she was gone," Mia continued, her breathing accelerating.

I waited a few seconds in silence anticipating in horror.

Mia blurted it out, "I tried to save her, but I couldn't. I was not strong enough to pull her out, and she drowned", she added, bursting in tears. "She was only 6 years old".

"Oh, Mia!" I cried on the other end of the call. "I'm so sorry to hear that."

As the train glided into the station, it coincided with the loud announcement blasting throughout the platform.

"That's why I _had_ to save Monica…Take care Julia, talk soon," Mia concluded the call.

I hastily boarded the train and sat down, still processing the surprising revelations. "Who could have foreseen this?" I whispered to myself finally grasping the weight of Mia's reaction during our earlier incident by the bay.

Sonia's Dilemma

A female professional finds herself working in a toxic work environment that is increasingly affecting her.

S ome people say that when you are working in a toxic work environment there is nothing you can do about it. "Put up and shut up or get out," it's the usual approach.

I wonder how many of you have ever worked in a toxic environment. That is a place of work where negative behaviours and conditions harm the well-being and productivity of the workers and affect not only the individual workers but the whole business.

Nobody wants to work in that kind of place, right? And yet, these places are more common places than we would like to admit. Look around you and think about it for a minute.

We all have heard of manipulations, bullying and harassment, discrimination, dreadful bosses or poor company culture in a workplace, where employees feel psychologically unsafe. To prevent these types of behaviours from happening, organisations usually have policies in place, or do they?

It all comes down to two simple truths: the toxic environment is either created and entertained by the top management in any organisation or it appears because they allow it to happen.

Here is an example of how this works.

Sonia was a tall green-eyed bright 40-year-old professional with over 20 years of experience in the adult education industry in Sydney. She was married, with two teenage children, and a husband who was busy trying to maintain the family status and advance his own career.

Sonia was determined to make things better and to improve the work environment that she was part of for everyone, as she truly believed it was possible. As any good manager, she supported her staff, coached, and mentored them, and provided them with assistance whenever they needed it while looking after the students and the courses and making sure that her department was achieving the organisation's business goals. These were the principles she conducted her work life by. She was prepared to put every effort she could muster into making the change and making better things happen.

When she took up the role of Operations Manager with "Global Education for Tomorrow", an ambitious private adult education organisation aiming for the stars, with a mission pointing to becoming the best education provider, she was convinced that she had arrived at the right place at the right time and that she could make a difference in the world, so she threw herself into her work with everything she'd got, and some. She learned the ropes quickly and started building a team whom she would train day after day to build a solid ground for future development. "Rome was not built in one day," she used to say to her staff. She made her mark quickly as she was experienced and knew how to handle staff and difficult tasks and she achieved results in a short time, within the budget. Therefore, Sonia was quickly noticed by the upper management in her first 6 months since she started her role.

One day, Johan, the Executive Director, approached her in the office and invited her for lunch the following day. Sonia accepted it not knowing what to expect.

Time flew quickly, and here they were face to face, Johan, and Sonia, at a café near their workplace in CBD, Sydney, on a beautiful day of March 2021.

"Sonia, how have you been?" asked Johan with a big smile on his face.

"A bit fake that smile," Sonia thought, but answered: "All good, thanks for asking Johan."

"Tell me Sonia," said Johan, "what can I do to help you in your new role?" Johan asked.

"I've been in this Operations Manager role for 6 months now, so it doesn't feel like a new role to me anymore", Sonia replied and smiled back at him.

"Yes, time flies pretty quickly, doesn't it?" added Johan. "Still, if you were to ask me only one question today, what would that be? Johan pressed on.

"Well," she said, "Now if you insist, I do have one question for you…," Sonia continued.

"OK, let's hear it," Johan encouraged her.

"I have this casual staff member who is not pulling his weight, and every time I'm trying to help him to perform his task he refuses my help, and then he still doesn't complete his task" Sonia explained.

"I've tried to help him so many times, but he was not interested, he just wanted to do as little as possible. This, of course, has a negative effect on my whole team. They all jump in and do the work for him, but this needs to stop."

"And what's stopping you from laying the ground rules and giving him an ultimatum?" Johan enquired.

"Well, I reported this to my Business Director, my direct reporting line, a few times by now, but there was a certain resistance to do anything about this case, I don't really know why, so I eventually stopped bringing it up. However, it's been affecting the work of my whole team, including their morale", Sonia said.

"Sonia, you have everything you need to make that decision on your own. Why don't you just go and do it yourself?!", Johan concluded.

"OK, I wasn't aware that I could make this decision myself, I'm happy to do it as I believe this is the best way to go in this case, thank you for your support," Sonia exclaimed, feeling relieved.

Soon after this conversation, the Executive Director excused himself and wished Sonia good luck.

In the following days, Sonia felt empowered by this conversation with Johan and proceeded to implement all the decisions she saw fit in her managing role for her department and kept her Business Director informed. Textbook management stuff.

Days turned into weeks and months and before she knew it, she was approaching the end of her first year of employment at "Global Education for Tomorrow" delivering great results.

Everybody seemed to be very happy with the year's outcomes and some managers even received bonuses. However, Sonia was not one of them, despite her achieving the goals. She put it down to being a new member of the company and thought she should wait a bit longer, that was all.

Then, when the yearly appraisals came by, she put together all her answers with documented data, as was required by the appraisal form, and added some suggestions for improving the overall business. She knew what could be done to advance their courses. For some reason though, her appraisal was delayed. Several months later, her appraisal session was finally scheduled. She was happy that she could finally have a say in the matter.

"Great work, Sonia!" the Business Director congratulated her. "You've proven yourself to be a great asset for our organisation. How did you manage to set up such a great team in your department? They are very happy with you, you know?"

"Sir, I really believe in what I do, and I make sure that everyone is well looked after and listened to," Sonia answered with pride.

"Keep it up!" came the answer. "We encourage all our staff to do better, and we make sure that their retribution is based on merit and correlated with their tasks and the complexity of their role, but at this point in time the organisation is not in the position to make any adjustments for you", he added.

Sonia understood. She's been passed on due to some organisational struggles. Or so they said, until she found out that other managers from similar departments who had not achieved their objectives but were connected to the top management level in different personal ways had been offered pay raises despite the circumstances mentioned to her.

She decided to let it go and chose to believe what she was told, for her own peace of mind.

In the following weeks, she noticed that employees from other departments were leaving their jobs almost every week, which was putting a lot of pressure on the existing staff who had to pick up the slack. This raised some questions across the board. Why were they leaving? Nobody knew. Initially, she didn't think much about it until one day when one of her closest staff's words resonated in her ears:

"I am still here because of you Sonia, I enjoy working with you. You stand for what's right and you are fair; otherwise, I would have been long gone by now." This thought made her take a closer look at what was really happening in the organisation, and everywhere she looked she saw unhappy people. "Well, that's a clear sign that something is not quite right," she thought. Wholeheartedly, she took it upon herself to find out more and fix it if she could.

The answers were always the same, staff were tired, working long hours every day with little or no break, no appreciation and low pay. Moreover, they felt trapped and thought there was nothing they could do. There was this expectation of delivering the results no matter what…but these expectations were not the same for all of them. That realisation made things difficult for Sonia. How can she address that unhappiness when the ultimate decision-making was not hers?

"Everybody knows that happy staff make things work well for everyone", she pondered. "Why can't anyone see this but me?"

She tried talking to some managers of the respective departments, to gauge their reaction to their own staff leaving and to her surprise, they didn't seem to care much. They believed it was not their responsibility to address staff concerns, which puzzled her. If issues were not dealt with, they would perpetuate, and the unhealthy cycle would continue. "Easily preventable if anyone cared", she contemplated.

After a while, she started noticing how some staff were taking leave more than usual. They needed a break. Nothing wrong with that, but when they came back the volume of work had doubled, as no one was able to deal with their work when they were not there. True or not, that leave was causing a lot of pressure on the full-time workers, more work for them. Management for some reason was oblivious of the situation, so it became a standard practice.

The continuous staff turnover seemed to be going unnoticed for a long time until Sonia decided to do something about it and raised it with her director. He turned around and told her plainly:

"This is not your concern Sonia," he concluded in their one-on-one meeting.

Sonia disagreed but kept quiet as he signalled the conversation was over.

It was by this time that she started to develop nightmares.

She enquired discreetly about the company's Human Resources services available to staff, and soon learned that there were none. Every manager was supposed to compensate for those human resources actions as part of their role, even if they were not qualified on the matter, and they had to deal with it for their own staff's wellbeing.

She was surprised, so she enquired with her director if there was any strategy that could be put in place to incorporate a proper human resources department or at least a unit in the overall organisational chart considering the medium-large size of the organisation. The answer was short: there was no need for a strategy. The organisation could function without HR to keep costs down.

She wouldn't let it go yet and she asked her boss if there was any sort of assistance available for staff who display high stress levels due to current workloads and ever-changing objectives outside the organisation, as most companies have similar services in place, and she was informed that there was no such service as it was not considered important. So, Sonia, stubborn as she was, went on to read more about the WHS Act, and learned that the Act was actually addressing the matters regarding staff wellbeing. It became very clear to her that the company chose to ignore them.

One summer morning, one of her staff reported to her being distraught and explained tearfully how she was verbally abused by another department manager for something she didn't do. Sonia straight away intervened and called a meeting with the alleged bully, and after a robust conversation with the respective manager, it was agreed that if a conflict situation with one of her staff would arise again, the matter would be conveyed to Sonia directly, so she could deal with her staff separately, to protect their wellbeing. She mentioned this incident to her boss, as per company procedure, but she already knew the answer to that. It was short "Deal with it," she was told. End of discussion.

At this point, Sonia became concerned about what other compliance issues might have been overlooked by the company's management, which could have put at risk the actual existence of the organisation, if the practices were not addressed properly, and guess what? Unsurprisingly, at this stage, she learned that there were several other breaches in their short-term/long-term action plans.

That didn't sit well with her, and she raised her concerns with her director once again but was ignored.

It was hard for her to admit at this point that her values were no longer aligned with the company's values, and she started experiencing lack of sleep almost every night.

And she was still receiving an increased number of tasks every day which prompted her to question if this was done deliberately to her, or it was just a result of poor management. She could never prove it either way, but that made things even more difficult for her and her stress levels went through the roof. "How is this possible to happen to me?" she argued.

When she realised that her department did not have the adequate resources to manage the excess business requirements continuing to flow into her department, she asked for more staff, but her request was denied. "Mission impossible," she concluded.

Not knowing what else to do, she turned to her General Practitioner. He checked her vitals and determined that she was in need of a long-term treatment due to the work pressure she was under for such a long period of time, as he discovered that she was at risk of having a heart attack and/or a stroke.

Still, Sonia was determined to overcome the hardships she was facing, and started the treatment believing that it was her own fault that she developed the health condition.

One day, she tried to talk to one of her colleagues and shared some of her concerns, but the conversation went sour very quickly, the other manager pretending she didn't understand what she was saying. Sonia felt alone and abandoned.

She turned to her husband for help, but the financial pressure of the house mortgage finished that dialogue very quickly too. She could not afford to quit her job, she needed to put up with it and keep her mouth shut. Not exactly the kind of answer she was hoping for.

Over time Sonia noticed that things at work were changing significantly, and unfortunately not in a good way. The upper management could not make up their mind on what they wanted to do which meant a lot of back-and-forth actions and changes of direction, from one day to another. Getting the job done was becoming more and more difficult. That level of indecision from above translated into more working hours every day, 8 hours a day turned into 10 hours or 12 hours a day, without any sign of slowing down. It was expected of managers to work long hours and without pay, there was no other way.

"This is what all organisations are going through," Sonia justified it, "so there is no point in saying anything," she convinced herself.

She was knowledgeable and efficient, and her staff followed her lead, and tasks were getting done properly and on time, but at what cost?

For Sonia, it felt like nothing was ever going to change. At least not in the way she thought they should. The top-down communication was always poor, and she felt trapped. Nobody can read minds. And then when the blame game began, she knew they were on a downward-spiralling pathway.

The students, who used to complain a lot before Sonia took up the management of the Operations department, were now over the moon with the service provided, and they were kindly passing on great feedback about her and her team to whoever was willing to listen. However, all that good news somehow eluded the upper management's ears.

Sonia, once again, did not make any fuss about it and she continued working 10-hour day shifts without complaining, to get things done and to ensure the students were happy with the assistance and their results. Complaining was not in her DNA.

One day though, she noticed that other similar staff in other departments were not treated in the same way as her, their workload was far less than what was coming her way.

This wouldn't have been a problem in principle, as Sonia was used to high volumes of work and could resolve things in no time. She was happy to do her job without advertising her efforts to the upper management level, until one other day, in a meeting, when it became clear that the volume of students and information that she was expected to manage was three times more than anyone else's in the room. So, this time she decided to raise her concerns and provided some statistics to back it up.

"Yes, it seems like you are having a bit more on your hands," the Business Director admitted, but "what exactly would you like us to do?", he enquired.

Sonia couldn't believe that reply came from a higher-up ranking officer, who knew exactly what was going on.

"I would advise we split the workload equally among the 3 departments, we have all the data here, and it would make sense to reallocate these tasks evenly, so they get done on time and everybody has a fair share", she added.

"I guess we can do that," the Director agreed. "I'll get back to you with the new allocation shortly."

"Thank you," said Sonia, feeling somewhat uneasy with the situation. "Why do I have to bring this up with all directors in the meeting, when the matter was known for months and could have been resolved a long time ago?" she reflected to herself.

After a couple of days, the Director's decision was passed on, and she learned that the reallocations still did not reflect an even number of tasks across all managers, as agreed in the previous meeting. Sonia and her team were still asked to handle double the number of tasks than another manager in the same team.

She pondered with the idea of pointing it out but convinced herself that this would not be a wise thing to do, and it would just attract more negative attention on her. Especially because the Business Director was well-connected to the Executive Director. "All this office politics. Keep quiet, better safe than sorry," she thought.

There was more that she needed to learn about the business in general she thought and the underlying connections before she could try again to level it.

She soon found out that one of the managers in that group was a direct relative to the Business Director, so she knew now why the spread of work remained uneven. "Nepotism," she figured it out. So, she continued with her work and dismissed any other potential remedial action.

As time passed by, the circumstances in the education industry changed dramatically, and the student numbers registered with the organisation started to dwindle. The business suffered an unexpected financial blow.

"Anyone in this situation," Sonia thought, "would round up all their experts and brainstorm together to identify new strategies for the business survival". Unfortunately, that was not what happened at "Global Education for Tomorrow ", and, as things were getting worse, Sonia decided to put forward some of her own business initiatives and seek upper management's opinion.

That was easier said than done. Nobody seemed to listen or care for that matter for what she had to say. The initiatives were not passed on, nor were they discussed or explained, they were simply dismissed.

Perseverant as she was, Sonia tried again to discuss with her director, in a renewed attempt to help out, but he wasn't interested. She wouldn't give up, and tried to talk to her peers, but they were too afraid to say anything. They took the approach of waiting for instructions from above.

When that didn't work, she tried to reach out to the Executive Director, hoping that the conversation they had a year before might still hold water and he might listen to her. This last effort was to no avail. Soon she realised that all avenues were blocked, and she wondered what else she could do, as she was genuinely still believing that it was not too late to turn things around.

That night, when she went home, she felt really disappointed. Things were just not working. She went to bed and tried to put her worries out of her mind.

When she finally fell asleep, she had a dream. There was this voice that was telling her about the fact that her days with the organisation were numbered. The voice continued:

"The day you raised your initial concerns with your director, 3 months ago, and told him that you thought the decision-making process appeared to be flawed, he made up his mind that you were an inconvenience, and he would get rid of you. Having a different view than his was the end of it. He was not going to accept a woman telling him what he could do, so be prepared, all your knowledge and skills were written off in an instant, you will have to go," the voice warned her.

When she woke up the next morning Sonia knew the dice had been thrown. Her director's ego prevailed. There was nothing else she could do.

The last question Sonia was yet to answer to herself was:

"Shall I say anything about what happened in this organisation and risk not getting another job or shall I keep quiet? We all know what happens to whistleblowers," she reminded herself.

Sonia tormented herself over it for a while, sipping from her cup of coffee.

"Will toxic work environments ever go away?" she wondered on the way to the office to pack up her things. "Not if everyone decides to keep it quiet forever," she concluded, determined to continue her quest for justice.

What would you do in Sonia's shoes?

www.ingramcontent.com/pod-product-compliance
Lightning Source LLC
Chambersburg PA
CBHW060752180626
46818CB00002B/543